PEPPED UP FOREVER

Pepper Jones Series #5

ALI DEAN

COPYRIGHT

Copyright © 2015 Ali Dean.

✼ Created with Vellum

Chapter One
JACE

How did she do it? Pepper never ceased to astonish me. I heaved myself into my Jeep, my trashed muscles aching with the movement, and started the engine. The radio blared a pop song about mad love and I reached to switch the channel on instinct before changing my mind. Pepper probably loved this song. She'd always had a thing for the girly pop singers. As I rolled down the windows and pulled out from the parking spot, I took in the view of Duncan Peak, amazed I was standing on top of it earlier this morning.

Three years ago, Pepper ran that same trail and returned before eight in the morning. It took her two hours and it took me over twice that long. I wasn't even sure I was up for the drive home, and she went for an ass-kicking hike with me that same day. The girl was seriously strong. In every way. And my mission was to be more like her.

It wasn't easy.

A lump lodged in my throat when I passed the camping spot we'd stayed at the night before I started college. On that trip, there had been dozens of people. Last night, it was just me sitting at the campfire. Yeah, it was kind of lonely, but I had to start spending more time in my own head if I wanted to deal with my shit. Pepper once told me running was like therapy for her. She thought through everything, felt through everything, when her legs moved up hills and along trails. I was trying the running thing, but my muscles were fucking heavy. I wasn't all long and lean like she was. Still, when I stood on top of Duncan Peak this morning, my heart racing and my quads burning, I felt closer to Pepper than I had in over a year.

The downhill was the killer though. All the pounding ripped my muscles to pieces. But being out here in the middle of summer, with no distractions, it made me see the beauty in a way I never had before. The world's beauty was bigger than my pain, more significant than my mom's failures, and worth living for. I was finally starting to *feel* again. And shit, it was painful sometimes. Being ditched by my own mother as a little kid and then again as an adult, it was a kind of rejection I didn't want to endure, wasn't sure I would come out of it whole. I had, but some days it was a fight to keep living and not hide like I once did. On those days, I leaned on Pepper, even if she didn't know it. I'd think about what she would do, how she would handle it, and what she would want from me.

Annie had called me about a year after she left Brockton the second time. Well, she'd called a few times over that year, but this was the first time I'd answered. It was what Pepper would have done, I thought. Anyway, Annie told me she'd gone to rehab as a condition of parole, after spending a couple months in jail for possession – I told her good luck, but I didn't need her in my life anymore. It was the truth, and I didn't even do it out of spite. I had more important people to spend my time on, myself included. If I was going to work on being real in my relationships, I was going to choose who those relationships were with. And since I couldn't have one with Pepper the way I wanted, I spent time going back down memory lane, reliving the good times, I guess. It helped me see my old self through a new lens – a perspective that made me cringe at times, but helped me move forward in an odd way, too.

Long-distance running might not be the best training for football, and I was anticipating several days of severe soreness that would set back my workouts. But it was worth it. As I forgave Annie for not loving me like I wished she had, and forgave myself for being an asshole and ruining the best thing in my life, I knew why Pepper loved to run. It had healing power like nothing else.

PEPPER

On busy nights like this one, the end of my waitressing shift feels like the end of a long run. My feet ache, and I'm craving a shower and a bed. Most of the tables in my section are already closed out and I'm contemplating taking a bath when I get home, but Ruthie finds me by the computer closing out a tab, and judging by the curious and awestruck expression on her face, I suspect something has come up.

"Did you see the group of guys who came in a few minutes ago?" she asks.

I shake my head and continue punching in numbers.

"I put them in the back booth. I know it's not your section but one of them specifically asked for you."

I raise my eyebrows in question, but she just shrugs and grins before spinning around. "Couldn't say no, Pepper!" she calls as she walks away.

Sighing, I rub my face, wishing the place hadn't mostly cleared out so I could claim I was too busy to take another table. But I'm in no position to refuse. Ruthie is only a few years older than me, but she *is* the manager on duty tonight.

Sometimes I wish I had a boyfriend just to avoid the awkwardness of getting hit on at work. I'm a terrible liar, so I can't even fake it, like

Ruthie advised me to do. For a while after Jace dumped me, guys still stayed away. At the time, it didn't occur to me that boys didn't flirt with me much or approach me at parties. But the residual effects of being Jace Wilder's ex-girlfriend wore off eventually, and I had to learn to navigate the unavoidable attention. I'm nothing special, but college guys hit on everyone. They have remarkable confidence. It's like once they leave home, they're stripped of all their high school insecurities and suddenly believe they are capable of getting any girl's attention. Or maybe they just have false confidence when they drink, which is in most social situations, it seems.

I'm expecting a college guy, so when I find Clayton Dennison sitting at the center of the table, surrounded by his Rockies teammates, my steps falter momentarily before I'm able to regain my composure.

Clayton flashes the smile I've seen a few times recently on television and the fluttering in my stomach rises until I swallow it back down. I'm used to dealing with kind-of-famous people. But the only experience with fame I've had before doesn't extend much past Brockton. The nervous anticipation that swarms through me isn't because Clayton's watching me intently, but because he's surrounded by guys I've seen on ESPN, whose last names are worn on jerseys all over the state, the nation even. Sure, "Wilder" is quickly making its way to that status as well, but it's different with Jace. Everything's different with Jace.

When Clayton asks all the guys on one side of the table to slide out so he can greet me with a hug, I wish I'd made an excuse not to come over here. Now eight giant baseball players are scrutinizing me, wondering what my relationship is with their teammate.

"Um, what are you doing in Brockton, Clayton?" And why the heck are all your teammates here? "Isn't it the middle of the season?" Last I checked, major league baseball was in full swing in mid-July.

"We've got a couple days off, and I haven't been home in months. It's great to see you, Pepper, you look really good."

Ignoring that comment, I murmur, "Why'd you bring your teammates? You know in about twenty minutes everyone will hear you guys are here, and the place will be swamped."

Clayton just chuckles, like he's already so used to the fame it doesn't affect him. "It's even crazier in Denver. Just wanted to get away for a couple of days before we're back on the road. It's the only break we have for a while, and there's not enough time to go anywhere else," he explains.

Noticing he's a little too close, I take a step back and ask the guys for their drink orders. Clayton has flirted with me for years and it's never gone anywhere. He's the kind of guy who doesn't know how else to act around women, so I let him try to charm me, knowing he's harmless.

Sure enough, the restaurant goes from nearly empty to capacity in less than an hour. I'm always scheduled for the opening shift so that I can be the first one to leave and get home at a reasonable hour, but tonight Ruthie begs me to stay until the 2 AM closing. Ryan is one of the bartenders tonight anyway, and since he's my ride home and can't get off early either, I don't have a choice. The Tavern is more of a dining establishment, though it does have an evening bar scene. Still, the few times I've stayed past midnight it hasn't been very busy.

But it isn't every day a group of Rockies players shows up at a restaurant in Brockton, and I have to shove my way through people to get to the booth in the back. Clayton isn't exactly a close friend, and I'm sure my annoyance at him for requesting me as his waitress is evident on my face when I deliver another round of drinks.

"Pepper, you should sit and have a drink with us. I checked with Ruthie, she said you didn't have any other tables," he adds before I can protest. It's true, my section closed out for the night, even though it's packed now. People have to order at the bar, and Ruthie made sure my only responsibility is keeping the Rockies players happy. Apparently Clayton is already on a first-name basis with my manager.

But I don't want to argue with him or wrestle the crowds again, so I give in and let the guys make room for me in the booth. A couple of them already got up to work the crowds and flirt with women. Clayton slides his drink to me but I point to his water glass instead, and he passes it over without question.

"So, what's new with you, Ms. Jones?" he asks, close enough that I can hear him despite the loud voices taking over the restaurant.

"The usual, Clayton," I respond dryly. I don't understand his apparent interest in me. I used to, I think. At least, it always seemed he wanted to flirt with me to get underneath Jace's skin. Jace Wilder threatened Clayton's position as Brockton's golden boy – top athlete, most popular guy, ladies' man – but that logic doesn't apply anymore. For starters, Clayton doesn't even live in Brockton these days, and his rivals for affection and fame are in a larger arena. And then there's the obvious. I'm no longer Jace's girl.

For some inexplicable reason, he still takes a weird pleasure in bugging me, and I sometimes find it amusing. But I'm tired tonight, and the only joy in sitting here now is that I'm off my feet. I'd ask for a foot massage too, but I don't want to egg him on.

"The usual, huh? You mean breaking records and breaking hearts?" he asks with a smile.

"Just base training for cross season at the moment. And I haven't broken any records recently," I add. I've been a solid college runner for the past two years, but not the standout I was in high school. I'm hoping to take it to a new level this year. I'll be a junior, and if I want the sponsorship to keep doing what I love when I graduate, I've got to start breaking records again.

"And breaking guys' hearts left and right with your spare time?" He's relentless.

"There's a pile of devastated guys in my wake, Clayton," I humor him. The truth is boring.

"I'm willing to risk it. Want to hang out tomorrow?" he asks cheekily.

"No thanks," I answer without hesitating.

He clutches his chest dramatically and a couple of his teammates give him a hard time for being turned down. "It's not the first time," he admits to them. "I've been asking her out for years and she always says no."

One of the guys sporting a wiry beard and chubby cheeks offers me a fist-bump and a solemn nod. "Don't cave, Ms. Jones. Stay strong."

"Thanks," I murmur uncertainly.

"Women should never trust a rookie to the major leagues.

Newfound fame and monogamy don't mix," another dude with a huge neck advises.

A guy with caramel skin laughs at that. "Right, Mitch, you would know, wouldn't ya?"

The guys trade jokes about their reputations, and I feel like I'm being initiated as one of the players on the Rockies or something. It's seriously weird. Why should I be privy to this information? Shouldn't they be more discreet? I could be a reporter for all they know. But Clayton's invitation to join them must have meant something, because by closing time they're claiming they'll come to cheer me on at a cross meet this fall. Yeah. Right. They don't even seem drunk, yet are ribbing me like I'm just another dude.

I'll admit I'm actually kind of enjoying myself when Ryan comes over to get me. The place has cleared out, but Ruthie didn't want to disturb our special guests, even though she made the rest of the patrons leave promptly at 2 AM. Special treatment for special people, I guess. That must be a motto in the restaurant business.

I haven't had anything to drink, but my head buzzes a little when I slide out of the booth. I mean, I just spent over an hour conversing with Rockies players. Baseball isn't even really my thing, but maybe that helped my cause. Surely they get tired of talking about their sport *all* the time.

Clayton backed off with his blatant flirting, but I still expect some sort of invitation to drive me home, even if it's just a joke. Instead, after exchanging a few "Hey, dude, how's it going?" sentences with Ryan, he leaves me with a non-sexual hug. He must have decided it wasn't worth embarrassing himself again.

Ryan doesn't hold back his curiosity on the ride home. "Buddies with the Rockies team, Pepper? I didn't see that one coming," he teases.

Laughing, I agree. "Yeah, that was not a scene I expected to fit in with, but those guys are funny. Crude, but funny."

Ryan just shakes his head, laughing with me or at me, I can't tell.

"Does Clayton still have a thing for you?" he asks easily, like it's not a weird question for an ex-boyfriend, or any guy, to ask a girl. The ex-boyfriend thing isn't all that relevant at this point I guess, since it's been nearly four years, but I still shift in my seat, the question making me uncomfortable. It holds more weight than he realizes.

"I'm not sure he ever had a thing for me, Ryan," I admit.

Ryan swings his gaze from the road for a moment to shoot me a miffed expression. "What? I remember him trying to get your attention when you were with Jace."

"Yeah," I say on an exhale. Talking about when I was with Jace isn't as hard as it used to be, but it still brings a pang to my chest. "That was just Clayton being a macho dude who wanted to try pissing off Jace."

Ryan nods, contemplating this. "Yeah, well, he seems to still want you, Pepper. Just be careful, he's got quite a reputation."

It's hard to get annoyed with someone like Ryan, who usually seems well-meaning. "Really, Ryan, you don't need to play big brother here." With Jace and Wes, I already grew up with two guys trying to protect me. Turns out one of them was probably the most dangerous of anyone.

Ryan laughs good-naturedly. "Sorry − it was just a funny sight, seeing you at the booth surrounded by major league baseball players. I feel obligated to warn you, but I'm pretty sure you can handle yourself so I'll shut up now."

Rolling my eyes, I decide to put Ryan in the hot seat. "So, who's the girlfriend this summer, Ryan? I haven't seen you with anyone lately." It's a little offensive of me, but we've joked before about his inability to stay single for long.

"Believe it or not, no girlfriend at the moment."

"Not even a sort-of girlfriend?"

"Meaning?" he asks with a smugness that tells me he already knows the answer.

"Puh-lease, you haven't had a real girlfriend since Lisa Delany. You just call them that to be nice." From what I can tell, Ryan's pretty good at having long-term hook-ups; he was "with" my former cross captain Kiki Graves for several months, but I don't think either of them took it seriously. I've learned that very few people are in real relationships in college. Most people just hook up with the same person for a while until they have to choose between cutting it off or making it into something more committed. This is one of the many reasons I haven't been with anyone since Jace broke up with me. Casual intimacy doesn't make a whole lot of sense to me, and I'm not sure I could pull it off even if I wanted to.

Ryan's pulled up outside my apartment on Shadow Lane but I linger, enjoying our banter.

He smiles, knowing I'm right. "Still looking for the right girl, I guess. Want to give it another shot?" he asks with a wink, letting me know he's joking, but we both know the question isn't a light one. Not really. And I bite, because why not? Since we've become better friends again over the past year, I've wanted to clear the air at some point.

"Ryan, would you seriously want to try going out with me again? As a girlfriend, I mean. The casual hook-up scene isn't for me."

He blinks, taken aback by my forwardness. But I don't beat around the bush about feelings and commitments. After what Jace put me through, I prefer to cut through the bullshit and get to the point. Jace never gave me that and it sucked. Still does, if I'm honest.

"Why?" he asks, with suspicion or curiosity, I can't tell.

"Dude, we get along great, always have. We've got tons to talk about and we went out before, so obviously there's some attraction there. We're both single at the moment, so I wanted to ask, see what you really think about it."

He leans back in his seat and shuts off the engine. "What about you? Are you asking because you're interested? Because if not, this is a weird conversation."

"I don't know why, it just seems like something we need to talk about. Like an elephant in the room kind of thing. But you go first." It's a challenge, and Ryan's a competitive athlete, so I know he won't back down.

"It's probably no secret I held a torch for you for a long time. Even when I was with Lisa," he admits, glancing at me with an indecipherable expression. "And yeah, I think I could be with you. Like, seriously with you," he adds with a smirk. "Not just sort of. But I'm not crushing on you like I used to, you know? I admire you, and I think for a long time your rockstar running abilities had me a little infatuated." It's an interesting response, and one I find myself nodding to in understanding.

"Your turn," he prompts.

"Yeah, I could see us together," I admit. We both laugh. "This is so weird. It's like we're talking about two other people, not ourselves. But I *am* the one who asked, so," with a shake of my head, I continue, "I guess it just seems like we're better as friends. I'm sure we'd be a cool couple too, but the fact that we hang out all the time without the urge to jump each other says a lot. I think we'll both find the right person, and we won't be able to resist them."

"Yeah, you don't want to start a relationship with an 'I could take it or leave it' mentality," Ryan jokes. Yet his words are right on point.

The truth is, I respect Ryan as a runner, as a good guy. I recognize he's an attractive dude. But I'd get bored with him. We might be able to love each other, but it'd be so predictable and anti-climactic. There aren't any fireworks. Because I've seen fireworks between two people. Experienced them. Felt the sizzle and crack deep in my bones. It's awesome and terribly painful. Would I do it again? Or do I want something less earth-shattering, less heart-breaking?

Chapter Three

JACE

There was a time after we broke up that I wanted Pepper to see other guys. I wanted her to get over me and move on. I *thought* I wanted that. Until Annie left, the second time, I always wanted what I thought was best for Pepper. I wasn't always right about it, that's for sure, but my instincts have always been to protect her, make sure she's happy and safe. Ever since we were little kids. A little less than two years ago, that changed. My self-preservation came first. I knew I was hurting her. But I couldn't help it. It hurt too much to feel, and being with Pepper always makes me feel everything. The good, and the bad.

And when I eventually started to snap out of my self-imposed prison, a sick part of me hoped Pepper would see other guys just so she'd know that what we had doesn't happen with just anyone. I'd had enough experience to know that what Pepper and I shared is rare. It was extraordinary, and not something she would find again. But Pepper wasn't like other girls. She didn't need experience with other guys to know that I was it for her. I think she always knew. The girl just got it.

At least, that was what I tried to tell myself on nights I knew she was out, getting hit on, maybe meeting her new boyfriend. Because really, I might have just been telling myself lies. Maybe she would find something even better with someone else. It was so fucking confusing.

I wanted her to be happy. God, I wanted that more than I wanted my own happiness. I just hoped so bad she'd find it with me. And I had no fucking clue how to do that. We could barely even have a conversation anymore.

I was getting ready to turn in for the night, my body aching and tired from the run this morning, when I got a few text messages from people telling me about the Rockies team hanging out at the Tavern. Pepper waitressed there most Saturday nights, so of course, I had to drive over there. The parking lot was packed, and I didn't want to go in and deal with the crowds or upset her. She would've known I was there for her, and that would've made her uneasy. I had accepted that she didn't really need me, but I couldn't help shadowing her like a stalker, just in case. It gave me a sense of purpose. Made me feel connected to her.

One time I probably overstepped a little, but I liked to think I helped her out. A guy on the hockey team walked her home a few months ago from a party, and I followed them. I knew it was messed up, but I couldn't help myself. I couldn't hear what they were saying, but I knew Pepper and her body language said she wasn't into him. And he wanted at least a kiss, but probably an invitation to her room. She managed to leave with neither, but I could tell she was uncomfortable. The dude totally wasn't going to back down, I'm sure had plans to keep after her the next time she was out, so I had a few words with him, without Pepper's knowledge, of course. He didn't bother her again.

Anyway, Pepper with Ryan was a different story altogether. I knew he gave her rides home from work, but it still sucked watching her get in his Jeep tonight. Pepper liked Ryan, and he wouldn't hurt her, so I had no right to intervene. I just hoped she didn't fall for the guy again. Or maybe I did. He was probably perfect for her. Shit. And now I was sitting on the front steps at my dad's house on Shadow Lane, wondering what the hell she was still doing in his car and wondering if there was any logical reason I could fabricate for walking down the sidewalk in the middle of the night. It was taking a lot of self-restraint not to go over there and bang on the window. I had serious issues.

The front door opened, and I heard my dad behind me. "You okay, Jace?" he asked, his voice raspy with sleep.

"Yeah Dad, what are you doing up?"

"Got up to pee and heard you pull in, then saw you sitting out here, thought it was a little odd." He joined me on the stairs, and we sat in silence for a minute.

There was no need to explain my compulsive tendency to follow Pepper around, pretending I was her bodyguard or some shit. My dad probably already knew it anyway. Hell, he knew I was in love with the girl years before I figured it out. But over the last year I had gotten better about talking stuff through with my dad. Even when it seemed pointless, it sometimes helped me figure out why I did the things I did. But sometimes I could just have the conversation in my head. And I knew why I shadowed her like a stalker. I wanted any reason to be close to her, and that was the best I could do.

Still, when she got out of the car a moment later and walked into her apartment building, my dad elbowed me. "You don't have to watch her from a distance. Just talk to her."

"You make it sound so easy, Dad," I scoffed.

He shrugged. "It should be. You've been friends since you could talk."

"She doesn't want to talk to me. I was an asshole. I hurt her, Dad. Me being around doesn't make her happy like it used to."

My dad didn't respond, and I took his silence as acceptance. He agreed with me.

"It'll be a good thing when I leave next year," I added quietly. Unless I fucked up monumentally this season, I'd be in the draft next spring, and on an NFL team this time next year. But the thought brought intense melancholy because it meant I wouldn't be able to stalk Pepper Jones anymore. It was really messed-up shit.

"Jace, why don't you apologize?"

I looked at him, astounded. "I told you I have, Dad. I've apologized to her practically every time I've talked to her. I don't even know how to look at her now without wanting to say I'm so fucking sorry." My voice was rising, and I hated that I was losing my cool.

My dad just narrowed his eyes. "Yeah, I remember. And she said she forgave you, didn't she?"

I didn't answer that. She had *said* she did, but it felt empty. How could she possibly forgive me?

"Maybe it's time you forgive yourself, Jace."

"Oh come on, Dad. You sound like Dr. Phil."

"Yeah, well, neither of you will be happy until you do."

"And how will that make her happy?" I was practically growling.

He raised his eyebrows. "Once you forgive yourself for hurting her, maybe you'll allow yourself to admit what you really want, and maybe you'll actually get it."

I stood up. I'd had enough of his bullshit. "You're an expert in relationships now, Dad?" I asked, opening the door, ready to end this conversation.

"Not really," he admitted. "But you and Pepper are special. It's easy to see and it's hard watching you apart."

It was hard *watching* us? Try living it, knowing it was my fault. But I couldn't be mad at my dad, and I reached a hand out to help him up. He missed her too, and I didn't blame him.

Chapter Four

PEPPER

"A real stud muffin stopped by looking for you," Gran announces as soon as I open the apartment door, having returned from a run with Zoe Sunday morning.

"Lots of possibilities there, but if Bunny's never met him, that narrows it down," Zoe comments as she hands me a glass from the cupboard and begins filling hers with water. My best friend since our freshman year of high school, Zoe Burton is well-acquainted with the kitchen in my apartment.

"You didn't know him, Gran?"

"Who says I didn't know him?" she asks mischievously. "Oh, this is fun. Let's see if you can guess!" She rubs her hands together excitedly. It's really hard to take her seriously with the neon sweatband around her head. Not to mention...

"Bunny, are you wearing spandex?" Zoe asks with glee, poking her head over the kitchen counter to get a better look.

Gran shimmies her hips in answer. "Gotta keep this body looking tight for Wallace, ladies."

I groan. I could have done without that statement. Wallace is Gran's boyfriend. They've been dating for nearly two years now, and I'm starting to worry he'll put a ring on her finger soon. As much as I like Wallace, I hate change, and him being my step-grandfather would mean a shift in family dynamic, big time.

"So, you gonna guess who the stud muffin was or what?" she eggs me on.

For a girl who's been single nearly two years, and had a total of two boyfriends in her life, there's a fairly long list of men who may have stopped by my front door. But none have a seriously romantic interest in me, I don't think.

"Was it Wes?" Zoe asks uncertainly. My heart sinks. I cleared the air with Ryan Harding last night, maybe it's time I do the same with Wesley Jamison. For Zoe's sake. I swear the girl thinks Wes still has a thing for me, which is utterly ridiculous. He may have had a crush on me when we were kids, but it's been a really long time. I'm pretty sure the reason the two of them can't move to the next level in their non-relationship has nothing to do with me, and if she's using me as an excuse, it's time I call her out.

"Nope," Gran says, popping the "p" in satisfaction.

Humoring her, I ask, "Ryan?" He doesn't stop by much, but I could have left something in his car last night, or he might have to give me something from his dad, my coach. Who knows?

Gran shakes her head, the grin growing wider.

Zoe begins to list off every male friend or acquaintance she can think of in Brockton, and with each one, Gran continues shaking her head, practically vibrating with anticipation.

Sighing, I finally realize who it must have been, and why Gran is acting so ridiculous. Well, more ridiculous than usual.

"Was it Clayton Dennison?" I ask, resigned.

Gran jumps in the air, pumping her fist. "Yup! Officially, we'd never met. But of course I knew who he was."

"I didn't know he knew where I lived," I grumble.

Zoe and Gran grin stupidly at me. Are they serious? "You really think it's a good thing that a major league baseball player was looking for me? Why?"

"Um, the question is, why *wouldn't* it be cool? You just told me about last night, Pepper. The guy is *interested* in you!" Zoe has been trying to get me to go out with guys all summer and every time she's on break in Brockton and, well, I'm pretty sure she and my college roommate Lexi conspire about it over the phone even when Zoe's at Mountain West, two hours away.

Gran raises her hand. "I'm not saying you should marry the guy, but I think a nice date would be good for you."

My eyes widen. "Who said anything about marriage? And who even said anything about a date? Did he leave a message asking me on a date?" Before I can continue with my rant, Gran begins to answer.

"Well, no, not exactly, but I know men," Gran says smugly, and I cringe. "And he's going to ask. He left his number."

"Gran, the questions were rhetorical." It's really hard to be annoyed with Gran and Zoe, who seem to think that dating any good-looking guy "would be good" for me, whatever that means. Zoe isn't around Brockton much and doesn't go to UC, so she can't know that Clayton Dennison has a reputation as a player and that he actually told me once he used to take steroids. Gran wouldn't know about that either, but professional athletes aren't exactly boyfriend material. Heck, that's probably *why* she wants me to go out with him. Besides, Jace Wilder's track record wasn't any better when I started seeing him, and that didn't stop me.

Didn't turn out well though, now did it?

"Pepper? You still with us?" Gran asks, bringing me back to the moment. "I was saying that I told him you'd call as soon as you got back from your run. Here's his number." She hands me a piece of paper with a phone number scribbled on it.

"Well, don't go out with him tonight, Pepper. Grilling at Wes's place, remember?" Zoe reminds me.

Good. I like having a valid excuse. And then he'll be back on the road and I'll be in the clear.

After Zoe heads home, I take a shower before punching in the number on the piece of paper. Clayton answers on the first ring.

"Hi, Pepper," he says.

"How'd you know it was me?" I wonder.

"Lucky guess," he says. "How was your run?"

"Fine."

"It was really nice seeing you last night," he says smoothly. "It's been too long."

His words convey we're old friends, but we're not. Not really. We've had several encounters over the years – some meaningful ones, yes – but we've never intentionally hung out together. I'm not sure how to respond to his strange comment, so I don't.

"Look, I know you thought I was joking when I asked if you wanted to go out with me, but I wasn't," he tells me. Here we go again. But this time, the teasing note usually in his voice is gone, and that means I have to give him a serious response. "Can I take you out to dinner tonight?"

"I've already got plans tonight, Clayton," I tell him.

"Can I take you out another time, then?" he asks, without hesitation.

"Why?" I can't help it, I'm suspicious.

"Why do you think? Because I like you. I'm interested in you. I want to get to know you better," he says.

He sounds earnest, and I don't know what his ulterior motive might be, but I simply find it hard to believe he wants to go out with me, on a real date. He now lives nearly an hour away and is on the road most of the time. Even if he *is* interested in me, like genuinely interested, it doesn't make much sense.

"Clayton, I just don't think there's any point in that." For some reason, it's easy being candid with him. He's got enough confidence that I doubt I'll hurt his feelings. "I'm not going to sleep with you," I tell him. Because really, why pretend that's not what's going on here?

Clayton chuckles. "I don't remember propositioning you, Pepper."

Well, now that I've made it clear *that* won't be happening, he can decide if he really wants to pursue me. "You didn't, but I don't want to waste our time. We're busy people."

"What are your plans tonight?"

"You're nosy."

"Just curious."

"I'm hanging out with some friends."

"That's vague."

"You want to know which friends and what we're doing?" I ask, annoyance building.

"Just trying to see if you were lying about having plans," he responds. "Anyway, even if you don't want to let me take you out for dinner, you and your friends should stop by the Marriott tonight. My teammates you met last night are staying there and are getting a keg."

"The Rockies are having a kegger in a hotel room in Brockton?" I ask dubiously. I mean, I don't know what professional athletes do on their nights off, but hanging out at a local restaurant one night and drinking at a hotel another is a bit unexceptional. It's the same stuff I do with my friends. I would have expected something more glamorous from professional baseball players. Yet I suppose they are in the middle of the season. And the guys I met last night seemed remarkably simple. In a good way.

Clayton laughs again. "Yup. Probably by the pool though. I'm sure the hotel won't mind."

"Okay, we'll see."

"The guys asked me to invite you," he adds, and I'm surprised he's still making an effort to see me. Didn't I say I wouldn't sleep with him? Does he think he can change my mind? Did I just inadvertently make myself a fun challenge for him?

But when I finally get him off the phone, I forget about it, as I'm sure he will. It will likely be months, or even longer, before we run into each other again.

Chapter Five

JACE

I was anxious and excited when I pulled up to the Jamison mansion. Every time I knew I'd see her, I'd get nervous like this. It had been more frequently this summer than when we were in school. We had too many mutual friends in Brockton, when everyone was home from college, especially since Zoe and Wes were seeing each other. Pepper wasn't avoiding me like she did last summer.

"Hey man, you're early." Wes greeted me with a brief hug when I found him in the kitchen. I wasn't usually early, but he knew as well as I did that I couldn't help myself.

As we moved some food from the kitchen to the bar by the pool, Wes updated me. "I talked to Zoe earlier, man, and she told me Clayton Dennison's after our girl again."

Wes referring to Pepper as "our" girl didn't bother me anymore. I used to think he wanted her like I did and at one point, I think he did. But the dude was totally in love with Zoe Burton, whether he'd admit it to himself or not. And that meant his thing for Pepper was only that – a thing – fleeting and something that probably wouldn't have broken all three of us apart as I'd once feared. Sometimes I thought his thing for Pepper was only heightened because he knew it wasn't going to happen for him. Even back then, in junior high, me and Pepper being together some day seemed inevitable. I wished I hadn't fought it for so long.

"Jace, did you hear me?" Wes punched me lightly on my bicep. "You want a beer before you hear this? It's going to piss you off."

I wasn't as much of a hothead anymore, but Wes still acted like I was going to flip out sometimes. "Relax, man, I've learned there are some things I can't control anymore. If Clayton Dennison wants Pepper, I can't do anything about it. She's a smart girl. She knows his game." I said this, but I was mostly trying to convince myself of it, not Wes.

"You know he showed up at the Tavern last night with, like, eight guys from the team, right?"

"Yeah, I know." I was there, lurking in the parking lot. I've turned into such a weirdo.

"Zoe told me he stopped by her apartment this morning when the girls were out running. Pepper's place, I mean. On Shadow Lane."

He went to her home? "Yeah, toss me that beer," I said quietly. "What'd he want?" First Ryan, now Clayton. Both were guys Pepper could fall for. But Clayton was more like me, and that made me uneasy. He was a wild card, and I didn't trust him. Just like I didn't trust myself. No, that wasn't right – I trusted myself, I just knew I didn't deserve the girl. Shit, maybe my dad was right.

Wes handed me a cold bottle. "He left his number, that's all I know. But she's coming over with Zoe, and the Rockies go to the east coast tomorrow, so I don't think they made any plans."

After taking a long sip, I asked, "What do you think about Dennison?" It was an open-ended question, but Wes knew what I was asking.

"I think the dude has had a thing for Pepper since high school, man. And yeah, maybe he noticed her at first because of you, but I don't think that's why he's still interested."

I nodded in agreement. It had been over a year since I'd done anything to publicly say Pepper was still my girl, except for maybe those words with the hockey player. It hadn't been easy, but I felt I owed it to her, to back off and let her be. And it wasn't hard to believe even a guy like Clayton Dennison would be interested in a relationship with Pepper Jones. He hadn't had a girlfriend since high school, but he wouldn't be the first to change his ways for her.

My hand went to my chest, trying to rub away the ache. Wes put a firm hand on my shoulder and squeezed. I never would have let him see me vulnerable like this a year ago, but it helped sharing the heartache. He was my brother, and he carried a little of the pain for me. And I carried his.

Wes's Lincoln Academy friends, Forbes and Pierce, showed up first. The girls they hung out with in high school, Madeline, Serena and Emma, were no longer invited to Wes's place. Actually, they weren't really invited to any get-togethers in Brockton, though they had started showing up this summer on occasion. They were old news, at this point, and no one cared. I think people wondered if I'd be a dick and make them leave, but as long as they didn't hurt Pepper, they weren't worth the effort. And Pepper could handle them on her own anyway.

The Brockton Public girls arrived next – Kayla, Andrea, and Lisa – and they each gave me those looks I was familiar with. All I'd have to do was look at them for longer than a fleeting second and they'd be leading me to the pool house. But I wasn't in the mood, because no other girl was Pepper Jones. And I couldn't even pretend otherwise anymore. It just felt so wrong.

My buddies from high school – Remy Laroche, Connor Locke, Ben Hughes and Ryan Harding – came with a keg, and I started to wonder if this was going to turn into a big thing. I'd hoped it'd just be a few of us, and that maybe Pepper and I could really hang out. It seemed like an environment she'd be comfortable in, people she knew, and not so many she could totally avoid me.

The burgers were grilling, the music was playing, and Pepper wasn't here yet. I missed her, and the ache was so much worse than anything I felt when Annie left. It was a wonder to me I was too blind with grief to see what a foolish thing I was doing back then. But then I heard her laugh and saw her walking across the pool deck with Zoe and their tiny teammate, Jenny Mendoza, wearing a polka-dotted sundress and smiling happily, and I couldn't help staring at her.

I wished I had a right to go up to her and lift her in my arms, brush my lips against hers, and tell her how much I loved it when she laughed. But I forced my gaze away, not wanting her to see the longing, because it would make her uncomfortable. She didn't like seeing anyone hurting, even assholes like me.

There was adrenaline coursing through me now that she was here, near me. And when the girls approached the bar, I called out to them from the grill, asking if they wanted chicken or a burger. Pepper wanted a burger, and I made sure to cut an extra-thick slice of sharp cheddar for her and cooked the thing until it was almost black, just the way she liked it.

When I handed it to her on a paper plate a few minutes later and took a seat beside her on a pool chair, it almost felt like everything was back to normal with us. We were sitting beside each other eating burgers, surrounded by friends, and I was asking her how training was going, and she answered me in a way that told me she actually wanted to talk to me. Savoring her words, I tried not to fuck it up.

Chapter Six

PEPPER

"I've been sticking to Coach Harding's training plan, which is mostly just base mileage until late August," I tell him. Jace is familiar with running terminology, and he knows that during the summer we just build up our strength and stamina logging the miles, without any speed work.

"But?" he prompts, sensing there's more.

"But I want this season to be different. And I'm tempted to start adding workouts."

He doesn't say anything, just watches me.

Sighing, I concede, "I know that's not the answer, I've made that mistake before. But I feel like I have more potential, and I don't understand why I'm not reaching it."

"Do you trust Coach Harding?" Jace asks.

"Yeah," I admit. "I do. He knows what he's doing."

"Maybe it's all up here, then," Jace says, pointing to his head. It's not the response I'd expect. The only other people I've talked to about this – Zoe and Lexi – simply reassured me that I've done really well so far in college. I may not be quite the standout I was in high school, but anyone would say I've been successful. But Jace gets it. He knows what it's like to want to be the best. I know I'm capable of more, and that's why I'm frustrated. But if it's in my head, what do I do? I find myself asking Jace this very question.

"If that's the case, what do you suggest I do about it?"

Jace laughs, like the idea that he might have the answer to this question is ridiculous. "I can't tell you why you're holding back out there, Pepper. For me, it's usually fear of something. But I don't know what you're afraid of."

I just stare at him, blinking to confirm this is Jace Wilder speaking to me. He's not only conveyed that he's thought through his own mental holdups, but that his primary one is fear. He's admitting to introspection and weakness. I almost want to call him out on it, because it's such a breakthrough, but I snap out of it. We're not close friends like that anymore. I can't tease him about something so serious.

Instead, I just nod and glance away, uncertain about why I opened up to him in the first place.

He clears his throat, and I turn my head to look at him again. It's something I try to avoid, because Jace Wilder always takes my breath away. That is one thing that hasn't changed.

He's studying me, and I wonder if he wants me to ask what he's afraid of. The question is on the tip of my tongue, but it's my own fear of what his answer will be that stops me. Instead, I ask him about football.

It should be an easy subject to talk about, but it quickly ventures to the NFL, and I start to understand that this might be the source of some of Jace's fear on the field. Fear of injury. Fear of leaving Brockton, the only place either of us has ever lived.

Our conversation is interrupted before we can delve deeper than either of us are comfortable with, and I'm grateful for it.

Jenny Mendoza plops herself beside me on the chair, oblivious to Jace on other side of me. "Rollie and Omar are at the Marriott at the party of the summer that *someone* didn't bother telling us about." She pokes me in the ribs.

"What? I thought Rollie and Omar were coming over here," I protest.

"They *were*, until Omar heard the Rockies team was throwing a party in Brockton, and all his old high school teammates are going." Of course, Omar plays baseball, and I'm sure he'll be thrilled to tell his college teammates at State that he had a chance to party with major league players. Rollie is Omar's best friend, and Jenny's boyfriend, so he was probably torn. "So change of plans, I'm heading over there. Want to come?" she asks me.

"Nah, I'm good here," I tell her. It sounds like she already knows I was invited earlier, which makes me wonder if Clayton said something to Omar and Rollie. That would be weird, since I don't even think he knows who they are or that they're my friends.

"Oh, hey Jace." Jenny sits up straighter, having just noticed him in the chair on the other side of me.

"Hi, Jenny, how's it going?" he asks.

"Good." Jenny's self-assurance wanes a bit in Jace's presence. I imagine she still remembers him as an untouchable high school senior, or maybe she's just struck by his good looks, which leave the best of us speechless at times. Either way, it makes me smile. Some things never change.

"How's Rollie doing? I hear you two are still together. That's awesome," Jace says. Jenny glances at me curiously, but I'm at a loss. I have no idea how Jace knows this information or why he's asking about it.

"Yeah, long distance isn't so bad. He's home for summer and breaks, and in a few weeks, I'll be in Boston too," she relays happily, remembering herself again.

"That's great, Jenny. I'm happy for you two," Jace says with such sincerity I find myself looking at him again. "Are you planning on running at BU? You're going to Boston University, right?" he asks.

"How'd you know?" Jenny asks, unable to hide her pleasure that Jace Wilder knows about her life. He shrugs and she beams at him. "Yup. The BU cross team's really good. Not as good as UC, but they qualified for Nationals last year, so maybe we will again this year, too. It'll be so weird racing you again, Pepper! But on different teams."

I tear my gaze away from Jace and pull Jenny in for a side hug. "I'll still cheer for you, peanut."

Jenny rolls her eyes and hops up, declaring she's off to meet some Rockies players – oh, and see her boyfriend, too.

Unfortunately, once the guys hear about what's going on at the Marriott, they decide to relocate. Wes doesn't seem to mind, and I have a feeling if Zoe wanted to stay at his place, he would. But now that everyone else is leaving, I worry the only people left at Wes's house would be me, Zoe, Wes and Jace. And that would be incredibly awkward.

As I follow the music and sound of voices to the Marriott's outdoor pool and patio, I'm reminded of who will else will be at this party, and that awkwardness tonight is inevitable.

Chapter Seven

JACE

Someone must have thrown down some cash, because the entire main floor of the Marriott was packed with people. Guys hoping to hang with major league players, women hoping to flirt with them. And it wasn't just the Rockies players Clayton brought to town last night. It seemed most of the team was here now, having decided to make a wild night in Brockton. There was no way I would have come if it wasn't for Pepper. And I was surprised she came. This was so not her scene.

But her friends were here, and most of them were leaving in a couple weeks for college. I hoped that was the only reason. She wasn't drinking, as I watched her from across the pool. Judging by the way she was eyeing the water, I bet she wanted to go in, but no one else had yet. There was a volleyball net set up, and I decided to go for it. Before tonight, I might have thought she wasn't ready. I would have been afraid she'd turn me down. But she *talked* to me. Really talked to me. Without anger or pain underlying each syllable. Without trying to get away as quickly as possible. Maybe we were moving forward.

My palms were sweating as I made my way along the edge of the pool, trying to avoid eye contact with a group of women who looked ready to jump me. I was nervous. Nervous about asking Pepper Jones to play pool volleyball with me. But I was going to face it, even if it made me feel weak and pathetic. Because I wanted her. And it just might take these little steps, which felt monumental, to get there.

When I saw who had already reached her, and had his hand on the small of her back, I almost turned away. Was I too late? Had I waited too long?

But I kept moving, and found myself standing across from Pepper and Clayton, with Omar, Rollie and Jenny watching us intently. I didn't want Pepper to hate me more for stepping in where I didn't belong, so I tried not to overreact. I had no right to stop her from seeing someone else, if that was what she wanted. But she needed to know I was here. And he needed to know it too.

Chapter Eight

PEPPER

Great. Now Clayton thinks I've come to this party for him. He's found me, and he isn't hiding his delight that I'm here. I'm about to try to explain that my friends wanted to come. Can't he see everyone in Brockton between the ages of eighteen and forty is here? But then I see the unmistakable masculine stride coming closer, until Jace is standing right in front of me.

"Hi guys," Jace says with a lightness in his tone that belies the stiffness of his body. "The net's free and I was hoping I'd recruit some people to play volleyball with me." He tilts his head to the pool, his gaze lingering on me before moving to my friends. He doesn't look at Clayton, who has positioned himself a little too close to me.

I *did* want to go swimming. I wore my suit to Wes's with that very intention, after all. But since no one is in the pool here yet, I didn't want to draw attention to myself.

Omar and Rollie, who certainly can't be oblivious to the tension in the air, jump at the idea of hanging with Jace, whom they've continued to idolize years after graduating high school. And I take the opportunity before I can second-guess myself. We need four players, and that leaves Clayton out. Maybe this will send him the right message.

Jace is the first one to jump in, and I immediately know we're going to have an audience. When women see a guy like Jace in a bathing suit, they watch. When other guys see his athletic build, they can't help but admire. It's been a while since I've endured the attention that comes with Jace Wilder, but I'm surprised to find that I'm not annoyed by it. Instead, I strip off my dress and splash in behind him, resigned that he'll be my teammate, but excited because there's little doubt in my mind that I'll forget the audience and have fun.

I'm glad I wore a sporty one-piece because there's a lot of jumping involved. It's a huge pool and we're able to contain the game mostly to the shallow end. It's a serious workout, and as the points go back and forth it's easy to work with Jace as a teammate and temporarily forget our past. Omar and Rollie are athletic and quick, and since none of us have exceptional volleyball skills, that's all you need to make it a good game. Jace is the dominant player, but he lets me hold my own side, and doesn't try to take over the game like some guys would when playing with a girl. We'd probably be winning by a landslide if he did, but that's not the point. He knows I actually want to play.

When we finally win, I'm not sure how much time has passed, but Rollie and Omar want to challenge us to the best out of three matches. Instead, we hear people call out they want next game, and before we can protest, several guys are in the pool arguing over who gets to play winner. I recognize two of them from last night, and apparently they win the argument, because I find myself in a volleyball game against two Rockies players. It's the one with the huge neck, who I learned was named Mitch, and the other is Juan, whose golden skin attracts some of the female attention away from Jace.

But when my competitive spirit takes over, I forget where we are and who's watching us play, because we're actually beating two professional athletes. The rush I feel is almost as exhilarating as passing someone on the track at the end of the race. Mitch keeps trying to slam the ball to my side of the pool, since, I'll admit, I'm the weaker player. But I hold my own, leaping shamelessly a few times and getting my nose clogged. When we finally claim victory, I'm in serious need of some water. Of the non-chlorinated variety, that is. I find Zoe on the side of the pool with Wes beside her, and she heads off to grab me something to drink. Wes fist-bumps me for my badass playing, and behind us Mitch and Juan are getting ribbed by their teammates. And then I hear Clayton's voice, announcing it should be four on four instead of two on two. Before Zoe returns with my water, a new game has begun, and this time, it's not as much fun.

Clayton, Jace, and a guy I don't know are my teammates, and we're playing four Rockies players, two of whom I met last night, but I can't remember their names. Mitch and Juan have been sidelined, apparently. The whole thing has turned into a fairly serious sporting event, given that the dozens of people poolside are now watching intently. It's not so easy to forget my surroundings now, because Clayton is trying to get all up in my grill and it's pissing me off. He acts like he's being chivalrous when really, it's insulting.

Jace watches the situation, and he keeps opening his mouth to say something and then closing it. I don't get it. The old Jace would just butt in and tell Clayton to let me play, end of story. When Clayton dives in front of me to get the ball and ends up hitting it out of bounds, I'm about to yell at him myself, but Wes does it instead.

"Clayton, man, Pepper can get the shots herself. Give her some space."

Clayton doesn't get a chance to respond, because the next thing I hear is a wolf whistle, followed by the distinct sound of Bernadette Jones cheering, "Yay, Pepper!"

Seriously, Gran is here? This is when most girls would dive under the water and hide from embarrassment. But I scan the crowd and find her standing beside Wallace, who's nodding at the people around him.

"Who's that?" one of the guys on the other side of the net asks.

"That's Bunny," Jace answers, like it's obvious, like she's famous and everyone should know who she is. I love it.

The guy shrugs in acceptance, making me laugh. "Did you bring your suit, Gran? Want to play winner?" I call out.

Gran frowns with disappointment in her lack of preparedness. "This was spur of the moment. Wally got a tweet about this party while we were at Bingo, and we hightailed it over here!"

Wallace gives me a thumbs-up, and I grin back at him in approval. Well done, Wallace.

"So, where's the keg?" Gran asks. And with that, Mitch shows her the way, and I'm back to playing volleyball. My heart's not in it anymore, and I'm kind of relieved we end up losing. I'm ready for a drink, and my skin is pruning.

Zoe's got a bottle of water and a towel for me when I hop out. "Looking good," she informs me with a grin.

"Thanks," I grumble. We both know it wasn't my intent, but I've managed to garner attention. This would be my cue to head home, but with Gran here, I'm happy to stay.

"She's by the bar," Zoe answers my unasked question, pointing behind me. Sure enough, Gran's surrounded by shirtless men, her hands on her hips, arguing about something.

"Oh, boy," I breathe out, wondering what mischief she's stirred up.

She sees me approaching and ushers me over, apparently with the belief I can help her cause. "What's going on, Gran?" I ask.

"These young men here seem to think I'm not cut out for a keg stand," she huffs indignantly. "Wally, what do you think? Do you think it's my age?"

Wallace eyes her up and down before deciding on an answer. "No. I think they don't want to be bested by a woman, that's what I think."

A few onlookers laugh, but the guys standing around the keg glance at me for help. I can tell they're thinking that this is my grandmother, so obviously I'll be the first to talk her out of it. But they don't know Bernadette Jones, so instead I nod and say, "Well, fellas, is that it? Are you afraid my gran's going to last longer than you?"

A moment later, she's hoisted up by two beefy guys, and she's chugging beer, her legs in the air. She only lasts for a four-count, but she's set in motion another competition, and now the party has diminished to a true kegger, with guys challenging each other and counting off how long they can last. I know I'll be dragged into it if I stick around, so I leave Gran and Wallace to their fun and search for my friends.

I spot Jenny and Rollie by the doors inside. She's sitting on a bar stool and he's standing in front of her, head tilted as he listens to what she's saying. Ignoring the pang in my chest, I continue wandering behind the crowds lining the pool, watching whoever is still playing water volleyball. Zoe and Wes are still sitting beside each other with their feet dangling in the water, and though I'm sure they wouldn't mind me joining them, I'd rather not wiggle through people to get there.

At one point, I thought I was the lucky one in love. Jace and I were together in college, and we had three years in the same place ahead of us, with no major obstacles in our way. But things changed fast, and I couldn't have predicted that Jenny would follow Rollie to college, that Zoe and Wes would stay kind-of together, even if they have some issues to work through, and Gran would be in a long-term relationship too. Oddly, seeing the others together and happy is comforting, even if it hurts a little. It means love lasts for some people.

Clayton's back is to me as he watches the game, his teammates beside him. I don't want him to notice me, and when I see familiar faces standing a few feet back, I'm approaching them without overanalyzing it. Jace's head is bent over his phone, texting someone, when I join the group. Remy and Ben are beside him, and they greet me easily.

"This isn't what we expected," Ben says, gesturing around him. "You and Bunny turned it into a pretty cool party, I'd say."

I nearly choke on my water. "What are you talking about?"

Remy laughs. "It was all macho guys with fan girls when we got here, and I was ready to bolt, but now people are actually having some fun." He nods to the chanting crowd by the keg stand, and the people jumping in the pool.

"You didn't tell me you'd been practicing your volleyball skills all summer, Pep," Jace's voice rumbles beside me, and the normalcy of the moment strikes me. His voice is light and easy, approving and teasing, and I want to melt into his chest. When my body leans toward him of its own accord, I realize what I'm doing and take a steadying breath.

"Right. Skills," I say shakily. Jace Wilder still smells the same. Clean laundry, pine (his deodorant or aftershave maybe?) and just, boy, or man, or something tangy I can't quite put my finger on. It's really not fair how enticing he is.

"You've made some new friends, huh, Pepper?" Ben asks, nodding behind me.

I glance over my shoulder to where Juan, Mitch, and Steve – the one with the wiry beard who told me not to cave to Clayton – are standing around with several women wearing skintight minidresses.

Frowning, I wonder at their attire. "Is there a club at the Marriott I don't know about?" I'm only half joking. But really, people don't dress like that in Brockton unless there's a fraternity theme party or it's Halloween.

"They're just trying to draw attention," Remy says with a chuckle. "They've got to stand out. There's lots of competition." He smirks and I look around, realizing women have come in droves.

I shake my head in wonderment. Most of the Rockies players aren't especially attractive, and since these women don't even know them, it can't be their shining personalities that make them irresistible. "How much do baseball players make, anyway?" I wonder.

"A lot," Ben informs me. Remembering Clayton's plea for a dinner date earlier today, I find it even more suspicious that he's interested in me, given that he's by far the best-looking of his teammates and surely has his pick of women.

"But not as much as Jace here will be making pretty soon," a female voice sing-songs. It's Amelia Laroche, Remy's sister, whom I've met a few times. She's four years older than me, but judging by the way she's holding onto Ryan's arm, it seems the age difference between us doesn't matter anymore. Or the fact that Ryan is her little brother's friend. I glance at Ryan and try to smother my smirk. Looks like he'll have a "sort-of girlfriend" for the rest of the summer after all.

He fake-scowls at me and then I really laugh.

"What?" Amelia turns, smiling at me and assuming I'm laughing at what she's said. "You don't think Jace is going to make it bigger than all these Rockies guys?" She twirls her finger around. "Just you wait. He'll get more from one underwear ad than most of these guys get in a year's salary."

"Amelia, really?" Remy asks, his cheeks reddening at the thought of his sister ogling one of his best friends.

"Yeah, Wilder, can you ask about having, like, a co-model? I'll start working out and maybe we can pose together for a billboard shot?" Ben deadpans.

I let myself steal a glance at Jace, who's shaking his head and refusing to answer the question. Half-naked Jace Wilder on billboards does not make me happy. I'm still possessive about him, even though he's not mine.

I've only recently allowed myself to wonder about the rumors that he hasn't hooked up with anyone since we broke up. I haven't heard anything about him with other girls, which is odd, because girls don't keep it a secret when they get with him. But I haven't let myself probe about it, even to my best girlfriends. I was afraid people just didn't talk about him in front of me because they felt bad, and if he was with other girls, I didn't want to know. But recently I've heard the murmurings. People wonder if there's someone in secret, because he doesn't give women the time of day.

His eyes dart to mine, and when he catches me watching he looks at the ground, almost *shyly*. Who is this guy? The one who interacts so easily with women, drawing them in without even trying, seems unsure of himself in this moment. And what's more, he's *letting it show*. He's not hiding it with flirtations, detachment, coldness or any of the Wilder methods I've come to know over the years. The aching curiosity to reach out to him, tug his hand and dig through his layers is quickly pushed aside by the alarm bells ringing in my ears, screaming danger.

When Clayton Dennison steps between us, I'm filled with an odd sensation. A strange mixture of regret and relief.

Chapter Nine

JACE

I wanted to tell her, "Baby, if you don't want me modeling in my underwear, just say the words." But then I remembered she wasn't my girlfriend anymore and I couldn't say things like that. Still, I was probably going to dream about the way she looked at me. It was that same possessive feistiness she used to get when we were together and women tried to pretend I was single. It was one of Pepper's hottest looks, and it was only Clayton Dennison's annoying presence that snapped me out of my daydream.

"It's a Brockton Public reunion right here at the Marriott," he said. Amelia was standing across from me, and the way she was watching Clayton put me on edge. Her expression was soft and sharp at the same time, suggesting they'd probably been intimate but that she was harboring bad feelings about it. Most likely, she wanted more and he didn't. That was the classic story with a guy like Clayton, which I could understand well. Yet, I'd slept with Amelia my sophomore year of high school, when she was a college freshman, and she'd never looked at me quite like that. Remy probably suspected, but he didn't know for sure, and frankly, I didn't think he'd really care. His sister was three years older than us and he didn't have much say about who she slept with. Hell, she was flaunting Harding in front of us right now.

Still, I got the feeling she was wary of Clayton by the way she was watching his every move, and then I realized she was studying the way he was standing beside Pepper. He had positioned himself slightly toward her, not touching but indicating to any onlooker that she was with him, at least for the night. Pepper was oblivious. She didn't really seem to be listening as Clayton shot the shit with Remy and Ben.

"Hey, Pepper," Amelia said, getting her attention. "Want to grab a drink with me while the guys catch up on their high school glory days?" she joked. Right. For the Rockies pitcher, I'd say he was currently living his glory days. But now I was dying to know what was going on in Amelia Laroche's head, because she didn't even wait for Pepper's answer, just grabbed her hand and pulled her along. Unless there was a bar inside I didn't know about, they weren't getting a drink.

Clayton's demeanor shifted, and his eyes narrowed as he watched the girls disappear inside the hotel. An awkwardness settled between us, and the other guys shifted uncomfortably while Clayton and I shared a dark stare-down. I was so tempted to get into it with him, to warn him off, stake my claim, but I had absolutely no claim here, and going all caveman was entirely counterproductive. It would only have made Clayton want her more. And he wanted her, whether or not I was in the picture; I could see he still had a high school crush on her. The way he watched her during the game, tried every move to get closer to her, impress her. I would have called him pathetic, but I was no better.

And then Bunny and Wallace joined us, and I was forced to calm down and get ahold of myself.

"Hey there, Clayton. Looks like you found my girl after all," she said, giving him a playful nudge. By the tone of her voice, I had a feeling Bunny had something up her sleeve. "He stopped by our apartment looking for Pepper this morning," she loud-whispered to all the guys, making a point not to look at me. Bunny clearly wanted me to know that Pepper had other admirers, and she didn't realize I already had my informants.

Bunny wouldn't do this to hurt me, so all I could think was that she was trying to get my attention. Did she want me to make a move for her granddaughter? No way. She couldn't want that after what I did, how cruelly I broke up with Pepper.

But if that was her plan, the little lady knew what she was doing. Because even though I already knew Clayton was going after Pepper, now all my friends knew it was more than simple flirting at a party. And once they started in on me about it, I'd get no relief. Despite knowing what I was in for, I smiled, because Bunny had forgiven me. Not only that, she believed in me.

"I think he wanted to ask her on a date, Wally," Bunny said to her boyfriend, making sure we could all hear.

Wallace nodded dutifully. "Who wouldn't? Pepper's a gem."

Bunny snickered. I think she might have been a little tipsy. I'd have to check in with Wallace before they left to make sure he was good to drive home.

"She turned me down, Bunny," Clayton announced, and I was a little surprised he admitted this to all of us. I thought he had more pride than that. Though I supposed it wasn't surprising. Pepper was too smart to make it easy for a guy like him. He'd have to prove he wasn't playing her, and I didn't know if even then she'd be interested. I was starting to feel better, like maybe I had the upper hand here, before I remembered this wasn't a competition. Not at all. And in any case, I certainly wasn't going to be winning Pepper's heart back by watching from the sidelines.

"Oh, you keep trying. She's a stubborn one. Thinks everything through before she does anything. I try to get her to live by the seat of her pants, like me," Bunny said matter-of-factly, "but that ain't her style."

"Whose?" Amelia asked. "Pepper's?" She was alone and I vaguely wondered where Pepper went, but my thoughts lingered on Bunny's words. Did she really want Clayton to keep trying for Pepper, or were her words directed at me? That woman was rarely subtle, but when I was the subject, the message seemed more cryptic. Or maybe there was no message at all.

"Where's Pepper?" Clayton asked Amelia, an accusatory clip in his tone.

"She decided to head home," Amelia said dismissively. I noticed she didn't have the drink in her hands that she supposedly left to get.

As usual, my heart raced in worry. "Who'd she get a ride with?" I asked. I wondered if I'd ever let go of this need to look after her, even though she'd made it perfectly clear she didn't need me.

"Zoe and Wes," Amelia told me. "They were heading out and she said she'd had a late night last night and was tired."

"Hmmm..." Bunny hummed loudly. She did this when she wanted people, or someone, to think about what had been said, though I wasn't sure why Pepper getting a ride with Zoe and Wes was crucial news.

"Something you want to share, Buns?" I teased, though I was genuinely interested.

"Well, she knew well enough she could have gotten a ride with me," Bunny pointed out.

"Yes, but you're on a date with me, and she probably didn't want to interrupt," Wallace reasoned.

"Perhaps," she reflected, like it was a mystery to solve.

I verified that Wallace would take Bunny home safely and then said my goodbyes, ignoring the knowing looks from Remy and Ben. My friends used to try to figure me out; they always knew Pepper was special to me, but lately I was being more transparent, and I wasn't even fighting it. I didn't realize how exhausting it was holding a wall up between me and the world until I started taking it down. Knowing my friends saw me and felt for me, it wasn't as scary as I thought it would be. Actually, it felt pretty good. I wasn't invincible. Why pretend otherwise? Especially when it came to one girl in particular.

If I ever thought it was Annie who had the capability to bring to my knees, I was so wrong. It was Pepper who stripped me bare and exposed me for who I had been. *Had been,* because I wasn't going back there. Pepper was the strongest of all of us, and I was happy it was her who ruined me. The truth was, she made me stronger for it.

Chapter Ten

PEPPER

I'm rarely alone with Wes and Zoe, but when I am, it's undeniable they are totally into each other. It's not just a for-the-moment thing either, time has proven that. During winter break my freshman year in college, Jace publicly declared that Wesley had been in love with me his entire life. Jace has never been the kind of guy who stirs up shit for no reason, and I thought I had to believe his words were the truth. Which had me in a panic for a number of reasons, and Zoe's interest in Wes was one of them. But even back then, I wasn't entirely sure how she felt about him. Zoe's always been a passionate girl, but she moves on quickly and in the end, she's a realist. So for a long time I thought she and Wes would fizzle out eventually, and one of the many concerns about Wes being into me would be moot.

But they didn't fizzle out at all. The more time they spent together during their school breaks, the closer they seemed to get. I stopped hearing about other guys from Zoe, and I never saw Wes flirting with other women like he used to. Still, they won't call each other boyfriend and girlfriend, and they pretend like they have an open relationship, even though they totally don't.

It's a wonder to me that Zoe might be held up by her belief that Wes is interested in me. I didn't think she could be so blind, but maybe it's time I say something to him, or her, about it. Only, what am I supposed to say?

They pull up to my apartment, and I decide I'll have to wait to get Wes alone sometime. "Thanks for the ride, guys," I tell them.

"You aren't going to tell us why you bolted out of there?" Wes asks before I can shut the door.

"Yeah, you practically chased us into the parking lot. What's up with that?" Zoe persists.

"You know me. I had enough of the crowds. Me and Dave need some quality snuggle time," I tell them, referring to my mutt, who sadly is the only male I spoon with these days.

They don't buy it, but they're more interested in getting back to Wes's place than giving me a hard time. Even though Amelia's words shook me a bit, I'm still smiling when I let myself into the apartment and flip through the channels for something mindless to watch.

Amelia took me aside and told me to be careful about Clayton. It was weird, for sure, because I barely know her, and it's not like his reputation is some giant secret. I asked her if I still seemed so naïve – I do know what he's like. But she shook her head and told me he'd wanted me for a long time. "He used to talk about you when he was in high school and even when he went to college, Pepper. I always thought it was weird, because you were so much younger than him. Look, he used to be a friend and I've seen him around since I graduated. He might seem harmless but I just have a bad feeling."

She was flustered, I could see that, and I wondered if she'd had a crush on him and had her heart broken. She couldn't know that I already knew about his interest in me going back to high school. He'd asked me to his senior prom when I was a freshman. And she might not be familiar with the history between Jace and Clayton. Jace had hooked up with Clayton's long-time girlfriend a week or so after Clayton and the girl broke up. That was when Jace was a high school freshman and Clayton a junior. Clayton had always felt competitive with Jace, the only other guy who threatened his reign in Brockton. But it all seemed like old news now. Yes, I'd sensed some tension between the two, but Clayton couldn't possibly still feel threatened by Jace, a college student who played an entirely different sport.

Still, I had to agree Clayton's interest in me was hard to explain, especially after seeing the crowd he and his teammates drew tonight. I'd taken the opportunity to split. My friends had paired off; even Gran was with her fella, and I wanted to avoid any drama.

When I hear a knock at the door, I'm tempted to ignore it. It takes me a moment, but eventually I get off the couch and check the peephole. And I stare. I step back from the door for a second, and Dave sniffs the door, wagging his tail enthusiastically. He's happy to see Jace. Probably because he doesn't have a very good long-term memory. Or maybe because Jace always feeds him from the table. Excuse me, Jace *used* to feed Dave from the table, when he came over regularly for meals. Jace only comes over now for a rare dinner when Gran extends an invitation to both him and his father. But he's here now, I verify again in the peephole. And he knows I'm alone, because Gran is at the party.

He doesn't knock a second time, but hesitates and then turns to leave. I swing open the door before he gets too far, and gesture for him to come inside. I'm not sure what to say, but he must be here for a reason.

"Want a drink?" I ask when he's inside. Why am I being so nice? Am I over it? Are we capable of being friends again? By the way the apartment suddenly feels way too small, and the way my thoughts jump to forbidden territory, I think I have my answer. I'm not sure I'll ever be able to be 'just friends' with Jace again.

He clears his throat, something I've noticed he does frequently now. It's like he's not sure what to say, and he's killing time. "Sure."

I open the fridge and gesture to the options. It's the same beverages we usually have, and he's familiar with the choices. He takes a beer and leans against the counter.

"I just wanted to make sure you were okay," he says. He sounds sheepish, almost embarrassed by this admission. It's not the confident tone he usually delivers statements like this one with.

"Why wouldn't I be?" I ask, genuinely curious.

He looks away, peeling the label on the bottle. "You left so quickly, I just... I don't know." He can't explain himself, and once again I'm struck by the urge to stroke his sharp jawline, to give some comfort.

He seems both more at ease and more uneasy than I've ever seen him before. On the one hand, he's not trying to hide anything or mask his emotions. He's letting himself feel. And what he feels is... nervous?

"Look, Jace," I try to reassure him. "I don't hate you. I'm not going to ream you out for checking in on me. I've told you, I forgive you for dumping me and being a dick about it, okay? I'm over it. You don't have to act all weird around me."

His eyes widen. I open mine wider too, as if to say, yep, I've become a little more forward. I'm not going to stand here awkwardly, pretending I don't know why you're so nervous.

And then he laughs, a full belly-laugh that's heavy with relief. "Wow, Pepper. You are something else."

Rolling my eyes, I grab a beer for myself and invite him to join me on the couch to watch *Seinfeld* reruns. I managed to keep it platonic with him for years when I was still attracted to him, so maybe there's hope for friendship after all. Do I really want that, though? Am I delving into dangerous territory? Sighing, I plop down on the other end of the couch, and decide to enjoy the company. It's not worth overthinking.

Chapter Eleven

JACE

I could tell she was second-guessing herself, and I was too. She had turned me away before when I'd tried to open the door again, but today she was giving me every reason to believe that I should keep trying, that being around me didn't hurt so much anymore. And I showed up because, yeah, I was a little worried, but also because I just had to see if the glimpse of *us* being cool together again was real. We had played like total badasses in the pool. Hell, we beat Rockies players. That meant we were good together, right?

But the energy on the couch was so palpable, it was impossible to ignore. She had to feel it too. There was a tension sizzling between us, a good one, filled with possibility, and I was trying my damnedest to respect the olive branch she'd extended. I didn't want to be that guy who was given an inch and took a mile. When I glanced over at her, there was no denying what the flush in her cheeks meant. She was squirming in her seat not because of what Kramer was saying on the television, but because she was finding the heat between us unbearable.

When she turned her eyes to meet mine, I swallowed hard. She wasn't even trying to hide the desire in her gaze. When she leaned the slightest bit toward me, I took it as an invitation, scooting quickly to her side of the couch and holding her face in my hands, bringing her lips to mine. Her mouth was warm and soft, and I couldn't tell if the sounds of surrender were coming from me or her. Pepper's hands wrapped around my neck, securing me to her, and I pulled her closer, so she was on my lap. It was the sweetest feeling, her body nestled in mine, and it was exactly the way it should be. So natural.

I'd wanted this forever, it seemed. The first kiss I'd had in so long, and I would've waited longer.

"Ahem!" Bunny called out. Pepper stiffened and I froze.

How had we not heard her open the door? Talk about being consumed in the moment. Shit.

Pepper's hands dropped from my neck and she shifted away before I could read her expression.

Bunny was standing over the couch now, arms crossed, with a huge, knowing grin on her face. "Should I pretend I didn't see that? It's been a while since I walked in on you two making out. Warms this little old heart."

Pepper groaned and hopped up from the couch. "I'm going to shower. I still smell like the hotel pool." I was glad she added that bit about the pool, because my insecurities flared up and for a second, I thought she wanted to wash any trace of me off her. And I was left with Bunny, who was tapping her foot and scrutinizing me.

When we heard the shower go on, she started in. "Well now, it seems you got my message. This wasn't exactly what I had in mind, but it seemed to be working out. Probably a good thing I got home when I did, though, huh?" she mused, and I wasn't sure if the question was rhetorical or not.

"You know what's going to happen now though, don't you?"

"What?" I asked, because hell if I knew the answer.

"She's going to put the brakes on. And you just let her, but not for too long, you hear?"

"How long?" I wasn't even going to pretend like I knew how to navigate this shit.

"I think you'll know," she replied before waving me off and going to her bedroom, leaving me alone in the living room, wondering what the hell I was going to do now.

Chapter Twelve

PEPPER

I'm still freaking out by the time I turn the shower off and wrap myself in a towel. My hand keeps going to my lips, reliving that feeling, and then I want to smack myself. I'm an idiot. Truly, a complete fool. How could I jump him like that? After everything? I've seen how he handles relationships when they get too close, and it's not pretty. I will not be a casualty of that. Again.

Resolved that I've given Gran enough time to scold him and shoo him out of here, I leave the bathroom and walk across the hall to my bedroom, shutting the door behind me. There's a gentle knock on my door a moment later and I tell Gran to come in, expecting a lecture of some sort. But it's Jace standing in my doorway. The first time he's been in here in a very long time, and I'm wearing a towel. Awesome.

"I'm sorry," he whispers, when he registers my surprise. "You thought I was Buns."

"I'm getting tired of you apologizing," I reply sassily.

He clears his throat, again, and probably suppresses the urge to apologize, again. "I was going to say I'm sorry for kissing you," he admits with a smile. "But now I don't know what to say."

"It was mutual. We both got taken by our history and forgot ourselves. It won't happen again." I try to brush it off. I'm inclined to blame it on having too much to drink, but we both know that's a lie. Neither of us drink much.

"Look, Pepper, if you don't want it to happen again, it won't. But, I miss you," he says. "Really miss you. Can we try just being friends?" He's begging me, and I'm torn. Wasn't that a pretty good demonstration that 'just friends' doesn't work for us? But the truth is, as disgusted as I am by his behavior during our breakup, he's a piece of me. Like family, I feel obligated to forgive him anything. And I have; I'm just not sure I want to put myself at risk again. I'm not sure I'd survive falling in love with him again. And I have a horrible feeling I won't be able to stop myself.

He sighs heavily. "You know I'm leaving in a year. Unless something wholly unexpected happens, I'll be moving after graduation. I don't know where, but it won't be Brockton."

"There aren't any NFL teams in Brockton," I agree.

"I probably won't even be in Denver. So, I know you're analyzing how we can be friends with our history, but you don't have to go too far into the future. We only have a year anyway."

When he says it like that, I feel a little foolish. "You mean, what damage could you do in a year?" I tease, but I'm choking out the words, suddenly filled with emotion. Sadness because he's leaving, and the chapter of Jace and Pepper in Brockton will be closed forever, no matter how it ends. Frustration because this isn't how I want it to end. And fear, most of all. Because I can't help myself and I want that time with him, yet I know a friendship with Jace isn't safe for my heart. But I smile anyway, conceding to his offer. I don't have the will to push him away.

———

When I wake up in the morning, I wonder if I imagined it all. What was I thinking? Friends with Jace? After I'd just kissed him like my life depended on it? Am I crazy? Shaking my head, I quickly change into running clothes and head out the door with Dave. I've got to get a hold on myself. Maybe he won't follow through. Maybe I can give him the brush-off, like he did to me once. No, I'm not vindictive like that.

The blood begins to flow as I jog through the neighborhoods, making my way to my favorite single track. But I still can't get my emotions under control enough to reason my way out of this. Actually, the only thing running through my head is how good his mouth felt on mine, his body, firm and strong beneath me. His hands holding my face like I was the most precious thing in the world. And then I'm reminded he can take that all away from me if he wants. If he shuts down again. And then where will I be?

Right, so I just won't kiss him again. Really, that was just a crazy reaction to being alone in a room with him for the first time since we broke up. I'll get used to it. Hearing someone behind me, I call Dave and move to the side. I'm rarely passed on this trail, but it could be Ryan or some macho guy trying to prove he can beat a girl. Instead, the person behind me doesn't pass but stops in front of me, and I'm pulled from my reverie. Well, actually, I'm pulled back into a different one, because it's Jace standing there with his hands on his knees, panting hard.

"You. Are. Fast," he breathes out. I giggle at the sight. His face is red from exertion and he's not trying to pretend he caught me without effort. It's pretty obvious he was sprinting.

"What are you doing?" I ask when he's caught his breath.

"I've been running in the mornings," he tells me, and I can't hide my shock.

"You hate running," I remind him.

"I used to hate it, but I'm starting to like it," he says easily. I must be giving him a dubious look because he raises his hands. "What? I'm serious. It's peaceful. Therapeutic. Like you always said."

"I'm not buying it."

"Fine," he says with a shrug. "I saw you go by my house and by the time I changed and was out the door I had to sprint like hell to catch you. I'm not sure I can jog with you, Pepper, I'm man enough to admit it."

Laughing, I don't argue his point. He's definitely got some extra muscle weight to carry, and that would slow anyone down. "We can try for a few minutes?" I offer, realizing I've got a chance to show that I *can* be just friends with Jace. I don't have to kiss him every time we're alone together. But who am I trying to prove this to? Him or myself?

"Ladies first," he says, gesturing. I'd rather he set the pace, since I'm not sure what he's up for. Sure, he's one of the most accomplished collegiate athletes in the country, but that doesn't mean he can keep up with me on the trails. As I jog at my usual speed and I don't hear him breathing too hard behind me, I realize he must have been serious when he said he's been running regularly.

We reach a look-out point and as I slow to a walk and approach the view, it amazes me I've never shared this with him. One of my favorite spots in Brockton, and he's probably never seen it.

"Have you been here before?" I ask.

"Only for the first time a few weeks ago. I jogged up here and I was pretty damn proud of myself. You've been doing it for years though, huh?"

We lean against a boulder and watch the orange sun shimmer over Brockton. I've taken in this view more times than I can count, and I'm startled by how intimate it feels to share this with him.

Gathering myself, I nod. "Yeah. I miss it when I'm at school. We don't usually run over here. And when we do, it's rarely first thing in the morning when the sun is rising."

"You still come back sometimes to do it on your own though during the school year," he says, and I swing my gaze to him, but he's looking out at the sun, and doesn't notice.

"How do you know that?"

"I've seen you," he says with a shrug. And the old Jace is back for that instant, because I know he's hiding something. But his self-assurance as we head back down the trail, this time with him leading, is comforting. I'd begun to worry he'd changed into someone I wouldn't recognize. But he's still confident enough to run with me, a challenge not many guys would take on.

And when we hit Shadow Lane and he invites me to breakfast, and to catch up with Jim, it's almost like we're back to our platonic days, when there was no promise of make-out sessions later in the day. Jim's got an odd day off between construction projects, so he's home, which saves us from being alone. He's not as surprised to see me as I expect, and we settle into our usual chairs at their little kitchen table.

"So you found out Jace is a runner now, did you?" Jim asks.

"I'm not sure I can be called a runner, Dad," Jace says between mouthfuls of waffles.

"You are if you want to be," I say with a shrug.

"You hear that," Jim says, pointing his fork at me. "The running guru says you can call yourself a runner. He's trying to convert me, too, but I get enough exercise on the job." Jim works in construction, but he's been a manager for years which, I'm pretty sure, means he's not doing the heavy lifting.

"Right, Dad," Jace calls him out. "You're going to get a belly one of these days. Playing ball once a week with the guys isn't going to keep you in shape."

Jim just smiles and takes a sip of coffee. "We'll see."

"Gran's been working out, Jim," I tell him. "You better watch out or she'll be able to lift more than you pretty soon." I don't tell him that her hand weights are four pounds each. Hot pink, too.

"If she runs, I'll run too. How about that?"

Jace and I exchange scheming glances. Jim should know better by now. Or maybe he secretly wants to become a runner. And just like that, I'm friends with Jace again. It's far easier than I thought it would be. Like coming back home, in a way. It should scare me, but it doesn't. As long as we can keep it to friends only, until he graduates and leaves, I'll be safe.

Chapter Thirteen

JACE

"You've changed," she told me later that night, as I drove her home from work. I was trying so hard not to rush ahead of myself, to be patient like Bunny advised, but when she said something like that, I wanted to spill my guts, tell her everything. We'd only reconciled yesterday, even if it kind of felt like we never stopped loving each other. As friends. Right, Wilder, get your shit together. She was attracted to me, I could see in the way she was looking at me, that hadn't changed. But if I moved too fast, she might run. She had every right to, and instead I had to show her that I was the one sticking around. I wouldn't run.

"Yeah? What makes you think so?" I was curious as hell.

She grinned coyly, and it made me light-headed. Focus on driving, I thought to myself, returning my gaze to the road in front of me.

"I changed my mind, I don't want to tell you – yet, anyway." Her response surprised me. Pepper rarely withheld information. It only heightened my curiosity, but I backed off. "I shouldn't have said anything, it just slipped out."

"Yeah, well, you've changed too." The remark flipped off my tongue easily, and I tried to rein in the flirtatious note in my voice.

"I have?" She sat up straighter, and I couldn't tell if she was amused or unsettled by my statement.

"You're bolder and more confident. You've always known who you are, but now, you're just rocking it." It was the truth, and I found it was easy to pour this part of my soul out to her, because it didn't mean I was making a move, and it needed to be said. "You don't second-guess yourself," I continued, but when she let out a little noise that sounded like laughter, I glanced in her direction. "What? Is that not true?"

"I second-guessed us being friends just this morning." My chest tightened at her words.

"And now?"

She sighed, almost happily. "It's good. Let's roll with it." I was filled with so much joy at her words, I almost pulled off to hug her. Just to wrap her in my arms and thank her for having such a fucking big heart. To forgive me and let it be. But instead I nodded and cleared my throat as I turned onto Shadow Lane.

"What else?" she asked. "What else about me has changed?"

I was idling outside her apartment, but I was in no hurry for her to get out. "You're even more direct. Like that – you wanted to know, so you just asked." I thought about how to say this. "But you're also harder to read, for me, at least."

She leaned back and crossed her arms. "Even though I'm more direct?"

Running a hand through my hair, I nodded. "Yeah, like, you get to the point, but it's almost intimidating." I chuckled to myself. Shit, I *had* changed. I never would have admitted this to anyone, let alone the girl herself, a year ago. "Your emotions aren't right there, at the surface and easy to see and touch, like they used to be."

Pepper's face scrunched up, but, just as I'd said, I couldn't tell if I'd offended her. It hadn't been my intention. I was only trying to be more honest with her. With myself. With everyone. It was the only way to have healthy relationships. Still, if I jeopardized this newfound friendship...

She nodded, accepting my words. "Well." Her voice was hushed. "It seems like we've traded places a little bit then, huh?" She opened the door before I could respond but I quickly leaned over the passenger seat to prevent her from closing it.

"Pepper?"

She turned. "Yeah?"

I started to say it, but stopped myself. She narrowed her eyes, somehow sensing that the apology I'd uttered over and over was on the tip of my tongue. But instead, I told her, "Anytime you need a ride back from work, let me know, okay? I'm only doing a few jobs for my dad this summer, so aside from training, I'm usually free." My social schedule wasn't what it once was and I was rarely out in the evenings.

"Thanks. Ryan can usually drop me off when he's working though, and I've still got my bike."

"I'd rather just drive you than have you bike, especially at night." I didn't touch the Ryan bit, even though my jealous side was screaming to say something.

"I wear a helmet and I've got a light." She didn't hide her amusement at my protectiveness. One day back in her life, and I was already trying to tell her what to do. I had to remember my place.

"Okay," I relented, though it made my chest constrict. It was simply against my nature to let Pepper do something potentially dangerous, like bike at night, without trying to stop her. But I did it anyway.

"*Okay?*" she echoed dubiously.

"If you'd rather ride your bike than call me for a ride, that's okay." It sounded forced, even to my ears.

Sighing, she waved goodbye. "See you later, Jace."

Was I imagining it, or did she sound disappointed? It didn't matter, because the sound of her saying my name would never get old. Ever.

Chapter Fourteen

PEPPER

I jog to the UC cross course today. I don't even realize where I'm going until I'm on the course, running over the grassy knolls through mile one and onto the wide dirt path where the course flattens out for a half mile. It's strange, running the racing route by myself, without teammates or competitors alongside or spectators and coaches shouting from the sideline. It's quiet and still, and all I've got are my thoughts, which instantly go to whether or not this will be my breakthrough collegiate season. After all, it was my junior year of high school when it all came together for me.

Jace told me I'm bolder and more confident, and that I don't second-guess myself. When it comes to my interactions with people, he might be right. However, on race days, I might start out positive and upbeat, but it's a flimsy optimism that crumbles as soon as it's challenged. And I don't know how to change that. In this moment, as I let my legs propel me down a hill and leap over a fallen tree, I'm itching to race and test myself. There's a need in me that won't go away, that demands to be heard. It wants to find out just how fast I can go, and how hard I'm willing to push myself. I don't just want to be another great college runner who trained hard and raced well. I want to be the best I can possibly be, and I want to win when it matters the most.

The exhilaration from running settles as I make my way home, channeling that energy and determination into safe-keeping. Now isn't the time to prove myself. It will come. Instead, my thoughts shift to Jace. One week of friendship with him, and no major issues. Aside from the kiss. Right, so it was more than a kiss. It was... intense. But I'm not thinking about that. Because he's changed, and in some ways, it's easier to be friends with the new Jace. He's not quite as mysterious. He lets me in. And it's not just me. His vulnerability is more visible to everyone. Yeah, he's still got that untouchable aura about him, but he's not afraid to let the world know he's breakable. He broke. And put himself back together.

But I'm trying not to overanalyze him or us or any of it, and instead I decide it's time to talk to Wesley. I'm not exactly looking forward to it, but it needs to happen, and it's a good distraction from everything else going on inside my head. I've got the day off from work, and I'd rather not spend the afternoon with my own thoughts. So, after showering and eating lunch, I call Jace to see if I can borrow his Jeep. Having another vehicle to borrow when Gran's isn't available is a benefit to being friends with my neighbor again. Jace has an afternoon workout but he can catch a ride with some of his teammates who are already back in Brockton for summer training, though it doesn't officially start for a few more weeks.

Be bold. Be direct, I chant as I pull into one of Brockton's fancier neighborhoods and park in the Jamisons' driveway.

As I approach the front door, Wes opens it with one of his signature lazy smiles and gestures for me to come inside. His laptop is open and papers are spread out all over the kitchen counter.

"Working on something?" I ask.

He scratches the back of his head as he opens the fridge door and hands me water. "Yeah, I'm playing around with some business ideas."

"Oh?" This is the first I've heard of "business ideas."

He waves off my curiosity. "Just having fun, researching for now. I'll let you know if it comes to anything."

"Right." I scrutinize him, and decide not to push it. Between construction jobs for Jim (his biological dad, which only his parents, me, Jace and Gran know about – oh, and Annie, but she doesn't count anymore), and spending time with Zoe, he hasn't been quite the social butterfly he usually is this summer. Zoe never mentioned Wes delving into the business world, and I wonder if she even knows. Maybe this is what he's doing with his spare time.

"So, what's up? You said you wanted to talk. You know those words make me nervous." He hops up on the kitchen counter and takes a sip of water.

"It's about Zoe," I tell him. It's not entirely, but that's the starting point.

"I haven't told her yet, or I'm sure you would've heard about it."

"Told her what?"

"About me and Jace. That we're brothers. How my mom had an affair, and now I have daddy-issues. All that crap." He says this all so lightly, like we're talking about puppies and birthday cake.

"Oh. Yeah, I know you haven't told her. That's not what I want to talk about."

He watches me, waiting, and I'm suddenly filled with nervousness. This could be a monumental mistake. What if I ruin everything? The balance in loyalties and friendships and relationships between all of us could so easily shift and slide until it's a giant mess. Or worse. Until it doesn't exist at all.

Be bold. Don't second-guess yourself. Be the Pepper that Jace thinks you are.

"Zoe told me this morning that you guys are going to study abroad together this spring."

He nods. "Yeah, we both got our acceptance letters to the program a few days ago. It's good news, Pepper. We're going to have a blast in New Zealand together. You should come visit."

Right. With all the extra cash and time I've got to travel the world. Zoe's scholarship covers most of it, but she's going to have to get loans for the rest. She probably never would have considered it if not for Wes's influence. But I'm proud of her. Still, this conversation needs to happen.

"Did you know that Zoe still thinks you have feelings for me?" I finally blurt it out. He leans back, mild surprise showing in his expression, but I don't think it's because of what I've asked. He knows. He's just surprised I brought it up.

"Is that what she said?" he asks.

"No, she's never said anything. But I know her, and I know you. And I see you two together. Neither of you have been this way with anyone else. But she doesn't see it, and you don't either," I point out, before getting back on track. "She doesn't see it because of what Jace said that night at your mountain house. And because of who you were in high school, and because you and I are close, and it's hard for others to understand that without making assumptions." I stop myself before I say too much. Maybe I've already crossed a few lines, but it needs to get out there, into the open, if two of my best friends are ever going to move forward in their relationship.

"Back up a second. I talked to her about what Jace said. The very next day, I told her it was bullshit, that he was just hurting and lashing out."

"So, you never had feelings for me?" There it is. Plain and simple. I'm pretty sure I know the truth, but it's time for Wes to face it head-on. Admit or deny. Either way, he'll be forced to confront his feelings about Zoe in the end. And that's why I'm doing this.

"Fuck, Pepper, are we seriously doing this?" He's off the kitchen counter now, standing in front of me.

"Yeah, Wes, we are. It's about time, don't you think?"

He looks away, and runs a hand through his hair in that same way Jace does when he's frustrated or thinking something through.

"Yeah, Pepper, some of what Jace said that night was true. But not all of it," he says steadily, never breaking eye contact with me. "Yeah, I was totally in love with you but I moved on. Years ago, okay?"

"How long?" My heart is racing so fast, but I hold still, letting him talk.

He lets out a breath, and with it, a small, tired laugh. "In fourth grade, I told Jace I was going to be your first kiss, and he pushed me so hard I fell over. He told me you would never let me kiss you." He says this all with a smile; apparently it's a fond memory for him. "As we all grew up, I think I just saw how Jace looked at you, and knew he'd never admit it. He'd get so mad if I'd tease him about it, so I stopped.

But you were special to both of us, and I didn't know how else to translate that, especially when my best friend totally had it bad. I thought it was the same for me, and Jace and I have always been competitive."

He lets me absorb those words before continuing.

"He wouldn't tell you how he felt, even though by the time we hit high school, there's no way he could keep fooling himself. Maybe I wanted to push him to do something about it, or maybe I just wanted to piss him off and show him I could beat him at something, but either way, I told him I was going to ask you on a date."

Raising my eyebrows, I ask, "When was this?"

"Right before my freshman year of high school. I know, we never went on real dates then. Hell, I never did until Zoe. But with you, I told Jace my whole plan to romance you." Wes grins at me, but he shakes his head when I give him a questioning look. "And there's no way I'm telling you those plans. But yeah, Jace pretty much flipped his shit about that. He stormed out and wouldn't talk to me for a week. And I didn't know what to do. His friendship was more important than getting you to be my girlfriend. So I went over to his house, and Jim answered the door. He knew we hadn't been talking, and he brought me and Jace into the living room to talk. But he didn't ask us what we'd been fighting about."

"He told you he was your dad. That you and Jace are brothers," I fill in, the pieces fitting like a puzzle. The summer before they started high school, when they found out they were brothers, and when everything changed. We each went to different schools for the first time in our lives, but that wasn't the reason why we stopped spending all our free time together. I was. At least, I was a part of it.

"And then Jace beat the crap out of me, which I think he'd been wanting to do for a long time."

"Right," I breathe out heavily, recalling the fight I'd heard about before. "But then what? The end of your junior year in high school, when you guys started dealing drugs, and then stopped, and Jace and I got together your senior year." *When did you decide you didn't love me like that?* I'm not quite bold enough to ask the question that I really want answered. But Wes knows me well.

"I'm not sure exactly when I realized that I didn't love you like Jace did. Maybe it wasn't until senior year, when I stopped being so pissed at him, and recognized that my own feelings were wrapped up in a whole mess of other emotions. I wanted to feel that kind of love, but only because deep down, I knew you reciprocated it for him. And that's what I wanted. That unconditional, totally untouchable love for another person. You two had it for each other, and I guess I didn't admit it to myself until the two of you finally admitted it to each other."

I try to ignore the well of emotions threatening to erupt when he talks about me and Jace and our feelings for each other, and instead, I focus on Wes and his feelings.

"But you do have that, kind of. We all love each other, Wes. We try to make up for the parts of our own families who are missing. And we do a good job, most of the time," I add with a smirk.

"Yeah, well, I guess I realized that too. And maybe it wasn't until I met Zoe that I realized what I felt for you wasn't the same thing."

"So, you're saying you love her?" I spell it out for him, and it's easy to see the question makes him squirm. He hasn't told her.

"Yeah." He's almost mumbling, and I'm tempted to taunt him into saying it louder until I've got him screaming that he loves Zoe Burton, but I refrain. "You were the only girl I ever felt close to, who I felt really knew me, before her. I never wanted any of the other girls to know me beyond the fun stuff. But for the first time, I wanted to let someone in, and it got worse the more time I spent with her."

"You mean better?" Does he even realize how similar he is to his brother in some ways? The Wilder men seriously need to work on this whole opening up thing, beyond just to each other, that is.

"Better, worse. I don't know. It's hard letting someone in," he admits.

"Like I said, you have your own reasons for holding back."

"I'm not holding back," he protests. "I mean, look at me, I invited the girl to study with me in a foreign country. That's a big step. Huge."

Crossing my arms, I level him with a stare. "You know what I'm talking about. She doesn't even know where you stand."

"Well, maybe she should ask."

"Would you give her a real answer?"

He smiles sadly. "Probably not."

"I think you should tell her everything you just told me. Clear the air. And that part about how you realized you didn't have the romantic feels for me? The part where you figured it out because you met her? Really put emphasis on that."

"When the time is right, I'll spill all the beans, okay?"

"Yeah, well, I think the time has been right for a while, but I'm going to back out now, and let you take it from here."

He looks like he wants to say something, but he shakes his head instead.

I've got a feeling I know what, or who, he wanted to talk to me about, so I say my goodbyes before he can interrogate me on his brother. It was my day to ask the questions. His turn will come. For now, I've got a date with Clayton Dennison to get to.

Chapter Fifteen

JACE

She wasn't here and I tried to keep it cool. Roland Fowler was one of Pepper's good friends, and he was throwing a party, which wasn't a usual occurrence. She should've been here. Hell, that was why *I* was here. Rollie said the party was thrown together last-minute, so she could have other plans, but I didn't know what they would be, when all of her friends were here. She'd had the day off from work today, ran this morning, and then did some errands with my Jeep. When I got back from my workout, the Jeep was back in my driveway. Pepper never went running late at night, so unless she had big plans with Bunny, I was at a loss.

I'd texted her once and called her once, and I was trying not to bombard her, but I couldn't stop checking my phone every two minutes.

Her friends didn't know where she was, either, and that was making me start to worry. I just wasn't sure whether I was being unreasonable here. I wasn't her boyfriend. I wasn't her protector. Her friends didn't seem worried, so I shouldn't worry. Right?

When I spotted Zoe standing on the porch outside, I made a beeline for her. She was chatting with Dana Foster and Tina Anderson, two girls who'd always wanted to be friends with Pepper, if only because they thought it would increase their chances of getting to know me. For that reason alone, I didn't like them. Or trust them.

"Hey Zoe," I greeted her, ignoring the other girls. "Can we talk alone?" I asked.

Tina and Dana giggled uncertainly before I gave them a pointed glare. They gasped, and then giggled some more, before shuffling away.

"They haven't changed much," Zoe commented with amusement. "I'm guessing you want to know where Pepper is?" she asked, giving me a once-over. She wasn't checking me out, just letting me know she was watching me. Zoe had definitely lost the star-struck demeanor she used to have around me, which was refreshing. I liked that she got all mama bear about Pepper. I even liked that she didn't trust me. After the shit I had pulled, I wouldn't trust me either.

"Yeah." To my amazement, I sounded just as sheepish as I felt. I'd really lost my touch. Clearing my throat, I continued, "We talked earlier today, and she didn't say anything about plans tonight. I figured she'd be here."

Zoe shrugged, but the stiffness in her spine told me she was a little perplexed too. "Rollie decided to have people over last-minute. Nothing was going on tonight, and his parents are in Chile or some-where." Her eyes darted away from me, gazing out at the expansive backyard.

"I'm worried," I admitted. Confiding in Zoe wasn't easy for me to do. She was judging me right now, I could tell. But I had to choke back the urge to hide, and let her see me for what I was. I was terrified as hell to show her my vulnerability, but forged ahead just the same.

"She could be on a date," Zoe suggested, and the ragged breath she took after saying this told me she was still a little bit nervous around me. She was testing me, feeling me out, and I guess she was trying to be brave too, in a different way. I admired that. She was willing to let go of her perception of me as this untouchable celebrity in order to support Pepper.

"A date, huh?" Assuming she was messing with me, I couldn't help but smile a little in amusement. She crossed her arms and lifted her chin, making my smile grow. But it vanished with her next words.

"Clayton Dennison's been trying to get her to go out with him all week. He's back in town for a few days. My guess is she decided to go after all, and give him a chance. Pepper doesn't like letting people down."

"But she didn't tell anyone? She would have told you, right?"

Zoe shook her head. "Not necessarily. She probably didn't want me giving her a hard time about it since I've been wanting her to go out with guys and she knows how nosy I can be."

Well, shit. It was like she'd chucked a rock right in the center of my chest. And here I'd thought Pepper and I were finally having a break-through, all I'd needed was some time for her to accept it. I was an idiot.

"Oh." That was all I could manage. The old Jace would've moved into action. Yeah, I had confidence then, but I was scared as hell too. I would've tried to stop her, made my intentions clear, and I certainly would've gone face to face with Clayton. Actions that showed confidence to the world, but were totally rooted in fear. But now? I was the asshole who'd hurt her one too many times, and she was the girl who was stronger than any of us, and certainly smart enough to make her own decisions about who she dated.

The tightness in Zoe's posture softened, and she actually reached out to touch my arm. "Why'd you fuck up so bad, Jace?" she asked.

My fists clenched at her brutal honesty. She was not making this easy. Not at all.

"You don't think I should have this conversation with Pepper first?" I wondered. I'd played it out in my head over and over, just waiting for the right time to say it. But she hadn't given me a chance.

"Why haven't you?" Zoe challenged.

"I've tried. I don't think she wants to hear it."

"Yeah, maybe she doesn't."

"That means she doesn't really forgive me, even if she says she does, right?" I'd take any advice I could get, and Zoe surely had some insight.

"There's a difference between forgiving you as a friend, a guy she's always considered a part of her family, in a way, and forgiving you, like, with her heart, you know? That sounds cheesy as all hell," Zoe said with a roll of her eyes. "But maybe what I mean is there's a differ-ence between forgiveness and trust, and she can trust you to have her back as a friend, but not trust you with her heart. Get what I'm saying?"

Rolling back my shoulders, I nodded. "I get you." It might have sounded mushy, but there was a bitterness there that screamed truth. "So you think she should see other guys because there's no hope for her with me?"

"I don't know anymore, Jace, I really don't. You are not the same Jace Wilder as before, are you?"

I would've liked to tell her I was a changed man, because that was what she wanted to hear. In some ways, I was. It was a complicated question that deserved more than a yes or no answer. "I've always been crazy about Pepper, that's never changed." Zoe nodded, and I was glad we had that point clarified. "The truth is, I was afraid she'd hurt me, so I hurt her first. And I put on an act, pretended I didn't care about her feelings and that I wasn't affected by anything because that's how I wanted it to be. But that guy who acted like an asshole, he was never really me in the first place, even if I tried really hard to play it that way. I guess I haven't so much changed as much as I accepted that I'm done being a coward and acting like shit doesn't get to me, when it really does."

Zoe crossed her arms and tilted her head thoughtfully. "These are nice words, Jace, but that's all they are. What if something unexpected happens in your life? A tragedy you don't expect? Are you going to hook up with Savannah Hawkins this time and send a video of it to Pepper? You've shown you're capable of some pretty cruel stuff, buddy."

I flinched at her words. Savannah's obsession with me had put Pepper in serious danger. Savannah had spent her time behind bars, but she was on probation now and in treatment for psychological issues. Still, after I'd kissed Madeline Brescoll, a girl also responsible for hurting Pepper, in front of Pepper for the sole purpose of pushing her away, Zoe's words were totally warranted.

"I feel like I don't know that Jace anymore, Zoe." My voice was quiet, but I hoped she knew I was being honest. "I can't say I won't react badly to tragedy, should it happen someday, but I've learned that pushing people away isn't the answer, even if it's my gut reaction." I ran a hand through my hair and sighed heavily. "I haven't even told Pepper this yet, so I can't believe I'm telling you, but I've seen a counselor, and it helped. That's not the only thing. It didn't work like a magic wand, but losing Pepper definitely forced me to figure shit out, okay? So yeah, I guess I *have* changed. Or improved," I added with one of my old cocky winks, in a vain attempt to lighten the mood here.

Zoe's lips were pursed in a tight line, and I couldn't tell if she was about to ream me out or burst into laughter. Instead, she just opened her arms and beckoned me with her hands. "All right, asshole, gimme a hug."

Startled, I stepped forward and wrapped my arms around her slight frame.

"You forgive me?" I asked.

Before pulling back, she answered, "Forgive? Yes. Still working on the trust part."

I'd take it.

Chapter Sixteen

PEPPER

When I see Zoe and Jace hugging on the Fowlers' back porch, I'm immediately uneasy. They totally just had a heart to heart about me, I know it. And what's worse? It looks like he's got Zoe on his side now. Spinning back around, I decide I need a moment to gather myself. If they see me, they'll know I caught them. And I don't want to have a deep conversation with either of them right now.

The date with Clayton was... okay. I'm not really sure how to characterize it. He wanted to take me out in Brockton, but I didn't want him driving all the way up here for me because really I was just doing this so he'd get off my back. Well, maybe I want to prove to myself that I can see other guys. Maybe if I have a new boyfriend, I won't fall for Jace. Yeah, I'm not even going to try to lie to myself. If I'm seeing someone else, things will have to stay platonic between me and Jace. And with Clayton practically begging me to give him a chance, he seems the perfect candidate.

I borrowed Gran's car and we met at a little French bistro in a town halfway between Denver and Brockton. Amelia's strange warning echoed a little throughout our dinner date. But really, she wasn't telling me anything I didn't already know. If she was trying to hint that his feelings for me weren't real − that they were based on some high school rivalry with Jace – well, I was already clued in. And though she didn't come off as petty like Madeline Brescoll or crazy like Savannah Hawkins, I'm aware that plenty of girls hide their jealousy well.

So yeah, we had a nice dinner, and he was really quite the gentleman. It felt all sophisticated, dressing up, having a three-course meal, and chatting about things besides the latest frat party or hook-up scandal. Not that I'd been on any real first dates before, but it felt nice. He walked me to my car, kissed me on the cheek, and that was that. It wasn't awkward or anything, but it wasn't exactly electric either.

I know my views on these things are a little unrealistic after Jace, so maybe having that kind of chemistry right away isn't that important. Jace and I had been friends since we were in diapers, so we were bound to have a different dynamic. And Ryan and I had good chemistry too, but so much of that was because of our shared passion for running and our apparently mutual hero worship of each other's running résumés. I think that was a little skewed as well.

I want to talk to someone about what I'm feeling, but I'm not sure if Zoe will understand. She saw how I was when Jace broke up with me at the beginning of college, and her biggest priority is protecting me from heartbreak. So the lack of chemistry might make her think Clayton is safe for me, and I'm less likely to get hurt if he dumps me.

Ugh.

This is so confusing.

"Pepper? Are you okay? You are, like, totally spacing out." Dana Foster's voice pierces through my haze, and I realize I'm leaning against a wall, completely absorbed in my own head. I can be a real weirdo sometimes.

"Oh, hi Dana." I stand up straighter, and then see her sidekick, Tina Anderson, is standing beside her. "Hey Tina. How's it going?" I've seen them around a few times this summer, and it's no surprise they're here tonight.

Tina and Dana exchange a secretive glance and then they're tugging my arm and telling me they want to ask me about something. They pull me down the hall until we're away from the rest of the party.

It's hard to believe they've already heard about my date with Clayton. One of the other reasons I wanted to meet somewhere else was to avoid girls like Dana and Tina hearing about it and bugging me for details. But when Dana opens her mouth, it's not what I expect.

"So, we were wondering, is anything going on with you and Jace?"

Before I can answer, Tina jumps in. "We know you guys broke up, like, a while ago, but we haven't heard about him hooking up with anyone else, so we just wanted to make sure before we..." She drifts off and my stomach clenches. Are they kidding me?

"Before you...?" I have to ask. I just can't help myself.

"You know, see if he wants to have some fun with the two of us tonight?"

A sick feeling washes over me but I regain my composure before giving myself away. Tina and Dana have a reputation, after all, and I shouldn't be shocked.

"Um, no, we aren't together, if that's what you're asking."

"Do you know if he's with someone else? Because he really isn't being very receptive, and I swear, I don't think he's hooked up with anyone this summer."

"Or last!" Tina practically whines. Like Jace is some prize, and it's his job to keep the college girls in Brockton happy. For the first time, I feel kind of bad for Jace that he has to deal with all this attention. Especially if it's unwanted, which I really hope is the case.

"I'm not really sure," I tell them. I'm at a loss about how to handle these two. They've always driven me nuts with their social climbing agendas, but haven't they grown up at all since high school? Can't they see that their questions are insensitive and rude? Or maybe they're trying to make a point of some sort.

"Look, I've got to go," I say, suddenly overwhelmed. The inside of the Fowler home feels cramped and stuffy and I'm dying to get out of here. I burst through the front doors and before I can think it through, I'm driving back to Shadow Lane and changing into running clothes. Leaving Dave at home, since he already ran with me this morning, I take the bike path, which has some sporadic lighting, better than nothing and an improvement over just my headlamp.

There's too much panic and confusion coursing through me as I practically sprint down the path. It's heightened by the guilt I feel for trying to run through it. I haven't done this in a long time. Running on impulse like this isn't always healthy, especially at night, and when I'm already on a pretty demanding college training regime. But as I continue to move forward, and my legs find a rhythm in the summer night, my thoughts become less erratic and I begin to feel more centered.

I try to sort through what's bothering me. I went on a date. With a guy who is really hot, and seems to really like me, even if his interest in the past was a little sketchy. He's a somewhat famous athlete, so that's a little disconcerting, but I've dealt with this kind of thing before.

Yet, when I told him I didn't want to meet in Brockton because his fame would attract attention, he seemed pleased by my response. Pleased in a way that said he really likes that he attracts attention. Jace has never been happy about the way he pulls people in and turns heads. He's good at it, and acts like it doesn't bother him, but he'd rather be inconspicuous. So yeah, Clayton's a little different in that way. Plus, when I learned on our date that he played for a AAA team in Austin, Texas last season, he seemed surprised I hadn't followed his career, and even a little offended. Maybe once you reach that level of fame, you just assume everyone from your hometown is paying attention. Maybe there's nothing wrong with that assumption. Still, it kind of rubbed me the wrong way.

I decide I'll give Clayton another chance. One more date, and then I'll know if I'm into him or not. It's not fair to compare him to Jace off the bat like this, and it went well for a first date. The way he listened to me intently was really sweet, and he did rescue me from Savannah Hawkins not once, but twice, back when I was a senior in high school. He's a good guy.

Having resolved that, I feel better as I turn around and jog home. I'm still uneasy about Dana, Tina, and other girls. What does it mean that he hasn't been with any of them? And why do I care so much?

Chapter Seventeen

JACE

When Pepper hadn't shown up to the party by 11:00, I decided to head out. Getting propositioned by Tina and Dana was a good indicator that it was time to call it a night. It amazed me that those two were still at it. I knew it had only been a few years since we all graduated high school, but I would've thought a couple years of college would have settled them down a little, given them a chance to grow up. But no, double-teaming the high school quarterback was apparently still a thing they wanted to check off their bucket list. Maybe I shouldn't have judged. Just because I had changed my ways didn't mean I should've expected everyone else to be right there with me. Not everyone hit rock bottom their sophomore year of college and was forced to reconsider their relationships with people.

I glanced up to Pepper's apartment as I drove past it. It was only last Saturday I ran up the stairs to check on her, and everything changed. As much as I wanted to do that tonight, I had to remember my place. Pulling into my driveway, a movement caught my eye in the rearview mirror. Somebody was out on the sidewalk pretty late, and after parking I jumped out to see who was roaming Shadow Lane close to midnight.

It was Pepper running down the street, a strong stride that told me she was trying to run through her emotions. My chest constricted in panic. Did something happen? It had been years since she'd gone on these impulsive runs, and only something major would get her doing it again. I knew that much.

"Pepper!" I called out, and she spun around. Even from across the dimly-lit road, I could see her face was flushed from exertion, but she didn't look distraught, and that eased my fear a bit. Still, she was on the way back from the run, which meant she'd already calmed down from whatever had prompted this late-night run therapy.

She stood completely still, her chest rising up and down the only movement. It was a weird sensation, walking toward her in the middle of the road late at night, with no one around. Somehow, it felt like we were going back in time, rewinding to when there was nothing messy between us, no regrets. Just Shadow Lane, the place we'd always lived, and the two of us, watching each other.

"Hey, Jace," she said, and I wondered if I was imagining how husky her voice sounded.

"What's going on, Pepper?"

She shrugged, and finally broke eye contact, once I was standing in front of her.

"Just needed a run. I wasn't out for long." She shut off her head-lamp and tugged it down from her forehead so it hung around her neck.

I didn't want to sound accusatory or admonishing, but I was curious. "Are you doing this a lot? Running impulsively?"

"No. This is the first time I've done it in years, actually," she admitted almost proudly. "With all the training I'm doing in college, it's not a good idea to add extra mileage."

We both remembered the last time she overdid it with her mileage; she'd ended up on crutches. It could have been a lot worse.

"Why tonight, then?"

"I didn't go for long." It wasn't an answer to my question, and I didn't think she was planning on telling me. Open and honest Pepper only went so far with me now, I guessed, and that sent a pang through me. She didn't trust me with everything, just like Zoe said. It was plain as day now. But I had to know if it was Clayton, and if he did anything to set her off, because she just told me she hadn't had to run it out in years.

"Where were you tonight? Rollie had a party and you weren't there." I was trying my best to sound gentle, but the irrational anger I felt toward Clayton Dennison, when I wasn't even sure that's who she was with, was simmering beneath the surface.

Sighing, she admitted what I already suspected. "I went out to dinner with Clayton."

Hearing it from her, such simple words, was excruciating. But this wasn't about me, not right now. "Did he do something to upset you? Is that why you were running?" Okay, now my attempt at gentleness sounded forced, even to my own ears.

"No, Jace, relax. He was a perfect gentleman, okay? It was the first date I've been on since, well, since you broke up with me, and... do we really have to talk about this?"

The lump forming in my throat was making it hard to speak. The words "since you broke up with me" rung in my head over and over. It didn't feel like I did that. It felt like someone else did. Some jerk, some idiot, who I didn't even really know anymore. And I kind of hated him. But what was worse? She didn't want to talk it out with me. She used to love talking things out with me. She never used to hide anything.

All I could do was shake my head. I wouldn't force her to explain. If he was the perfect gentleman, I had no reason to intervene. I wanted to ask her if she did this to hurt me. Why now? Why wait until we're reconciling to date again? Was she trying to get back at me? Was this her revenge? Because if it was, it was totally working. It hurt like hell. But that wasn't Pepper. She wasn't trying to hurt me, and that made it even worse.

Chapter Eighteen

PEPPER

It's been two weeks since my date with Clayton. He's had games either in Denver or out of state nearly every day, or else he's traveling. It's nuts. I'm beginning to realize that I'd have to be pretty committed in order to actually have this go anywhere with him. And to be that committed, I'd have to be head over heels for him, which it doesn't seem like I am, at least not yet. He calls and texts nearly every day, and even sends little stuff like flowers and teddy bears. He doesn't know that after the stunt Savannah Hawkins pulled, I'm not a big fan of flower deliveries. Still, it shows he's thinking of me, which is nice, I guess.

He's invited me to watch his games in Denver, and says we could meet up after, but I'm usually working, and driving an hour to watch a guy play and spend a little time with him is not really on my agenda right now. I'll go on another date with him, I've told him so, but it just hasn't happened yet. I've got a lot of friends I want to spend time with this summer, and going out of my way to make something happen with Clayton isn't a priority.

Preseason training starts in a couple of weeks, and while I'm excited to move into off-campus housing for the first time and start running with my teammates again, I'm going to miss my Brockton crowd. And, well, things have settled into something comfortable and almost normal with Jace, and I don't want to disrupt that.

I don't fight it when Jace starts to make his presence in my life habit again, like old times. I know it won't last anyway, with college starting up again. He stops by unannounced occasionally, and sometimes joins me and Gran for dinner, sitting in his old chair. When my shifts don't coincide with Ryan's shifts at the Tavern, Jace gives me rides so I don't have to deal with biking or borrowing Gran's car. The trail runs together are new though, and because of that, I'm not sure how I feel about it. Okay, honestly, I'm totally thrilled that Jace can go with me for my shorter jogs, but the fact that I'm thrilled also leaves me a little terrified. I don't want to give him too much of me. Still, I'm comforted knowing once preseason starts, there won't be any time for runs with Jace, so I'm not in too much danger.

Tonight, a big group of us is going to watch a Rockies home game. I waited until the last minute to let Clayton know we'd be coming. I didn't want him going out of his way getting us seats or anything, and I didn't want him trying to plan anything special with me afterward. If my friends want to hang in Denver after the game, and he wants to meet up with us, that's fine, but most of us aren't even twenty-one yet so we can't exactly go out to the bars. I'm pretty sure most of my friends have fake IDs, but I don't, so I guess I'm the party pooper. Zoe doesn't either; I suppose it's her way of acknowledging that her dad is, indeed, a cop, even if she defies his rules the majority of the time.

It's a Friday afternoon game, and we're squeezed into the Burton family minivan. This is actually Zoe's minivan now, because her mom got a new one to cart around her four younger siblings, and Zoe got this lovely hand me down. I'm sure Mr. Burton would not be pleased to know that there are eight of us squeezed into the seven-passenger vehicle: me, Zoe, Wes, Rollie, Jenny, Omar, and Wes's Lincoln Academy buddies, Forbes and Pierce. We're meeting Jace and his crew at the game.

When my phone rings and Clayton's name appears on the screen, I'm more than a little surprised. The game starts in thirty minutes, so he really shouldn't be calling me.

"You're coming?" he asks with excitement.

"Yeah, we're on our way. Shouldn't you be warming up or something? I heard you were pitching."

"Not until the third or fourth inning. Who are you with?"

"A bunch of people. We're in Zoe's sweet ride." I've told Clayton about Zoe and her minivan. From our phone conversations, he's heard the basics about my friends in Brockton, though he doesn't know any of them very well.

"I wish you'd told me you were coming sooner, I would've gotten you guys a box."

"Don't worry about it." It's tempting to lie and tell him this was a last-minute idea, but we actually decided a few days ago. Forbes's dad's company had all these tickets, and it took a little coordinating to get all of us off work at the same time.

"I'll see you after the game, right? What are your plans?" he asks.

"I'm not sure," I say hesitantly. "We haven't really decided on anything."

I hear his name called in the background. "I've got to get going, but I want to meet you later, okay? I can always drive you back to Brockton tonight. We don't have a game tomorrow."

"Yeah, we'll see. Talk to you later." I'm not sure why I'm so reluctant to spend time alone with Clayton. Most girls would be elated, wouldn't they? Maybe it's Jace's fault, and he's made me wary of all guys. There must be *something* wrong with me.

Wes is driving and from the passenger seat Zoe spins around and asks who I was talking to.

The music is blaring but Wes turns it down just as I answer, "Clayton Dennison."

And I can practically feel the weight of everyone's curiosity pressing on me now. I thought I'd been talking quietly on the phone with him. Zoe must not have been tuned in to the conversation in the back of the van, and was eavesdropping. I'm sitting behind her, so I guess she can't be blamed. But now everyone's going to know, and this is what I'd been trying to avoid. Oh well, it's not like they wouldn't have found out after the game anyway.

"You were on the phone with Dennison?" Omar doesn't mask his excitement. "Is he pitching tonight? Wait. Why was he calling you?

And this close to the game? Is something wrong?" Omar's definitely got a baseball crush on Clayton.

"No, he was just checking that we were coming. He might meet me after the game."

Omar's eyes widen and his mouth forms into a neat little circle.

"He's got the hots for our girl," Zoe explains.

"Zoe!" Aside from Jace and Gran, she's the only one who knows about the date two weeks ago.

"He's been sending her flowers and stuff," she says all suggestively, and I want to smack her on the back of her head. The traitor.

"It's nothing, seriously. We've only been out once, and I doubt it will go anywhere," I say, trying to tamp down where I assume everyone's heads are going. He is not my boyfriend. Not even close.

"Flowers?" Pierce asks with a smirk from in between the captain seats. He volunteered to sit on the floor. "Sounds like you got the dude wrapped around your finger, Pepper."

"Let's talk about something else," I declare. "What do you guys want to do after the game?"

"Well, if *Clayton* is meeting us, I'm sure he'll have some ideas," Zoe remarks. I can only catch the profile of Wesley's expression, and he's not giving much away. I wonder what he thinks about Clayton.

Rollie helps me out by listing a few places without a twenty-one and older entry policy. Jenny doesn't have an ID either, as far as I know. She still looks like she's fifteen in some ways, so I'm not sure how well it would work anyway.

"We don't need to worry about that if Dennison's meeting us," Forbes points out. "If we're with the team, no one's going to check IDs."

Sighing, I try to protest that I'd rather go somewhere legal, and I'm not sure we'll meet up with him anyway, but my friends are already imagining some epic night downtown with the Rockies. After meeting some of the players at the hotel party, the guys, at least, seem to think they are legit groupies or something.

I'm feeling agitated and kind of angry, though I'm not really sure why, when we find parking and walk a few blocks to the field. It's a hot day, and I'm committed to drinking water and staying hydrated, though a few of my friends already cracked open beers in the van. Between the extra passenger, the drinks and the fake IDs, I'm surrounded by law-breaking delinquents. But after purchasing a hot dog and smothering it with ketchup, I'm starting to shake my negative mood and get into the baseball fan mood.

Our seats are behind first base, and the rest of the crew is already there. Jace, Ryan, Remy, Ben, Connor, and the Barbies. In my head, I continue calling Kayla, Andrea and Lisa by the label Zoe gave them in high school. They all still rock the long blonde hair and girly attire, looking put-together in their Rockies shirts and matching shorts. It's funny that all of us hang out together in the summer now, when my friends rarely overlapped with Jace's crowd in high school. I never would have pictured this scenario four years ago.

The Barbies still act like they're better than me, Zoe and Jenny, but it seems petty and a little pathetic instead of intimidating and meaningful like it once did. I'm sort of glad Amelia isn't here, because I worried Ryan might invite her and she'd give me another talk about Clayton being a bad idea. People always want to give me advice for some reason. But I'm not as naïve and innocent as I look. I've been harassed and stalked by crazy people and I've come out tougher for it.

Our group ends up in the row behind Jace's, and I find myself staring at the back of Jace's head and admiring his broad shoulders, which seem to fill out more every year. I'm not surprised he's already chowing down on a cheeseburger and fries. The kid never stops eating.

"Want some?" he asks, tilting his head back and holding out his fries.

"Sure." I snag a few and lean over to dip them in ketchup. I ran ten miles this morning, and I'll admit, I eat almost as often as Jace does.

As I take in the people around us, I notice for the first time the jerseys with "Dennison" displayed on the back. It's an odd feeling, seeing his name worn by random people. He's someone important, and I almost feel like a fraud. Who am I to turn down dates with him? And why me, anyway? The jerseys must be new, since he only joined the team this year. When he steps onto the mound in the third inning and his name is announced, the odd sensation multiplies. This guy I just talked to on the phone is out there on the field, and thousands of people are watching him on their televisions. But instead of the pride I feel when I watch Jace's football games, which don't have nearly as many viewers, instead I feel a little queasy.

It's probably just the hot dog I ate earlier, but there's just something so off about Clayton's interest in me. He's too big, too, well, major league, for me. And even though Jace has that aura of celebrity about him too, it feels almost innate and natural to who he is, and there's a familiarity between us that will never exist with Clayton. But, I'll admit, he looks really good in his baseball uniform up there, and when the Barbies gush about it, I have to agree with them.

My queasiness subsides with the seventh inning stretch, and I sing along with "Take Me Out to the Ball Game," making me feel all patriotic and American. When my phone vibrates from my back pocket, I'm amazed to see it's Clayton. If he's texting me in the middle of a game that he's pitching in, maybe going on a second date with him is a bad idea. I already feel like things aren't going to go anywhere for us, and I don't think he's on the same page.

He's asking me to meet him after the game, and describing where I can find him outside the locker rooms. I'm uncomfortable splitting with my friends, but maybe I can count this as our second date, and then explain to him why I don't think we should keep doing this, whatever it is.

I want to ask Zoe for advice, whether I should just ask him to meet up with us later, but she's on the other side of the row. I don't want Clayton to think I'm playing games with him, and I don't want him distracted texting back and forth with me about plans, so I just type a quick "ok,'" and hope I can pull this whole thing off without any drama.

Chapter Nineteen

JACE

Pepper disappeared after the game. One minute, she was telling Zoe something, and Zoe was nodding, and the next she was gone. We were all standing around, deciding where to go, and then we were leaving, but Zoe didn't ask us to wait for Pepper. It wasn't a quick trip to the restroom, and I was pretty sure I already had the answer to her whereabouts without asking. All of her friends were shooting me hesitant glances, and I was practically certain she had plans with Clayton, and they were nervous about how I was dealing with that.

Well, the only reason I wasn't flipping my shit is I'd heard, from Zoe via Wes, that Pepper was not super into it. I was mostly annoyed with Clayton, who clearly wasn't reading her right, but then again, maybe Pepper was being too nice, which wouldn't surprise me.

It wasn't until we left the field and I walked right into ghosts from my past that I was actually grateful she wasn't here with us. Wolfe, Rex and an equally sketchy-looking dude were standing right in front of us, and Wes stopped in his tracks, having spotted them too. I knew they'd moved to Denver a couple of years ago, but I hadn't seen them. Wes and I kept track of them for a while after they messed with Pepper as a way to get back at us for not connecting them up with the gang who sold us drugs. It was hard to believe that guy who sold drugs and dealt

with gangs and dudes like Wolfe and Rex was me. It was like I shed
him a long time ago but he was still lingering in the shadows, taunting
me. I had made so many mistakes.

I glanced at Wes, and I could tell he was studying them, trying to
decide if their presence was a coincidence. When they finally noticed
us, there wasn't a whole lot of surprise in their expressions. Our friends
were getting restless beside us, but they seemed to notice at the same
moment that there was a reason we'd stopped, and it wasn't a
good one.

Wolfe lifted his lips, almost like he wanted to laugh at me, and it
made my blood go hot. I was the one with the upper hand here, not
him. Narrowing my eyes, I tried to convey the threat without words. I
had information on him that could put him away for years. Deciding
that I needed to know why he was here, and if there was any reason for
alarm bells, I stepped forward, and I could feel Wes at my side a
moment later. We had plenty of guys with us right now, though I
would've rather not gone there tonight.

"What are you doing here?" I asked, my voice calm and confident. I
wasn't afraid of these guys, I just needed to know their agenda.

Wolfe tilted his head to the side and looked at the group behind
me. He spread his hands. "Here for the same reason you are."

"Really?" There was no emotion in my voice, but the question
conveyed I didn't trust this guy for a second.

"It's been a long time, Wilder. We used to be buddies. I'm over our
dispute. We have our own thing going on down here, and your business
is old news." By business, he meant my dealing connections. I hadn't
kept tabs on Wolfe recently, but last I knew he was still involved in
that world, trying to climb the ranks in a bigger city. He'd gotten a
little smarter, but if he was still using, he wouldn't last much longer.

Rex shifted beside Wolfe, and the other guy with them was
glancing between me, Wes and Wolfe uneasily. He didn't know who we
were, and that told me enough. Wolfe hadn't prepped his sidekick
about me, and Rex looked like he wasn't expecting to see us, so this
wasn't a planned encounter.

Wesley drew the same conclusion, and when I gave him an
approving nod, he reminded Wolfe, "It's a good thing you aren't

causing us any trouble, because I've been dying to unload the evidence I've got sitting around on you."

We walked away then, and as we did the reasons why Wolfe was dangerous rested heavily on my shoulders. He had terrified Pepper one night, forcing her with him and other guys to a pool house during a house party, until we'd intervened, leaving all of us to wonder just how far he had been planning to go. And the video he sent, which had threatened to tear Pepper and me apart before we'd barely had a chance, still made me feel sick. But we'd overcome all that, so why was Wolfe's appearance making my heart race and my adrenaline pump? This was how I felt before a game, when my body was geared up for a challenge. Wolfe hadn't challenged us, and I didn't understand why I was reacting like this.

Was the unease that settled in my gut simply from the reminder of my past mistakes, or was there something more? I couldn't shake the feeling that I was missing something.

Chapter Twenty

PEPPER

Why did I agree to meet Clayton again? It's starting to get dark, and I'm waiting in this weird alley that's top secret, according to Clayton. He initially told me to go to the official exit from the players' locker room, and there were a bunch of reporters and fans hanging around. I'd felt pretty stupid standing amongst all of them, but then Clayton texted me to go to this back alley where most of the players exit in order to avoid the crowd. I'd feel kind of special being let in on this little secret, except there's no one else here and I haven't seen any other players leave yet. Which is probably a good thing, actually, because then they'd wonder what I'm doing here.

Zoe texts me that they are at a bar two blocks away, and not to worry because most bars don't start carding at the door until later. I'm not sure I want to ask Clayton to go there with me. It'll be weird with Jace and my friends there, not to mention all the randoms who will want to talk to Clayton. I'd rather get this second date thing over with and hang solo with Clayton for a little while before breaking things off. It's stupid that I'm even thinking about this as a breakup, when we're really not anything at all.

When I hear footsteps approaching from around the corner, I stiffen. I feel like I'm not supposed to be here, and I wonder if some security guard's going to pop out and yell at me. The last person I expect to see emerge from around the corner is Wolfe Jenkins.

"Pepper. Jones," he enunciates slowly. What the hell? I'm in a dark alley, with one of the scariest people I've ever encountered, and the way my body is shaking, I know this isn't some bad dream. It should be.

"What are you doing here?" He's at least thirty feet away. Why is he here, now, after years with no threats and no indication he would be back?

He shrugs. "I saw you leaving the game and followed you. It's like you were asking for it, leading me into this deserted alley."

I almost laugh at the absurdity of this moment. But self-preservation kicks in, and I spin to the door, for the first time trying it to see if it's unlocked. It's not. Before I can make a break for it and join the crowd by the other exit, he's behind me, lifting me and squeezing my arms so tightly I can't push free.

"Let go of me!" I shout. There are hundreds of people just around the corner and I yell over and over, certain that someone will hear me any moment and come running. But he's dragging me farther away even as I kick. I wish more than anything I was a bigger person right now so I could get him off of me.

He's grunting against my struggles, and I don't give up, but then he's shouting to someone else to open the trunk, and I hear voices that I can't decipher buzzing in my ears. There are two others, and one is vaguely familiar. My vision blurs as I fight uselessly and I don't know if it's from loss of oxygen or panic, but the ringing in my head is making it hard to focus. Wolfe's grip on me is crushing, and it's only getting tighter the harder I try to break free. Rex appears and tries to grab my feet, and I kick him away, a bizarre sense of satisfaction bursting through the panic for a moment as my foot connects with his head and he stumbles backward.

But then another guy, one I don't recognize, blurs into my vision, and before I can react, a sharp pain courses through my skull, and the world goes black.

———

Something is pounding on the back of my head when I open my eyes. Through hazy vision, I make out a concrete ceiling and a light bulb. Where am I? And then it rushes back, and my body jerks. The movement is painful and I cry out.

"Shhh..." Someone brushes hair away from my face and though I'm almost afraid to look, I dart my eyes to see who it is.

"What the hell?" My mouth goes dry. Clayton is hovering over me, and my head is in his lap.

"Relax. Stay still. I've got you," he says. And then I get it. He found me outside. They must have left me after I passed out.

"What happened?" My voice is dry, and it doesn't sound like me.

Clayton's entire body stiffens at my question. He croaks out, "What do you remember?"

I tell him. "Wolfe and Rex, these two guys who used to live in Brockton, they grabbed me and tried dragging me into a trunk or something. Another guy was there, and I think he knocked me out. Honestly, I have no idea what they were trying to do." Kidnap, or worse, are the only things I can think of. And though I'm sure it was rooted in a kind of twisted revenge, something holds me back from telling all that to Clayton. I should be relieved that I'm not bound and gagged in a trunk somewhere, but I still don't feel safe. I need to know what happened.

"That's what I saw when I came out to meet you," he says through gritted teeth, and I wonder if this all happened minutes or hours ago. He still seems to be pulsing with adrenaline. "I ran at them, and the guy holding you dropped you on the ground. You went like a sack of potatoes, Pepper, and I was terrified. I started to take them on but they ran scared. Juan and Steve came out as they drove away."

Juan and Steve. Caramel and beard.

"How long ago was that?"

"You've been out for half an hour."

I try to sit up, and Clayton helps me, but the room spins, and I have to lean back against the locker. I'm flooded with nausea and I quickly put my head between my legs to avoid losing the hotdog and fries I ate earlier. Was that just a couple of hours ago?

Clayton rubs circles on my back, and suddenly, more than anything,

I want Jace. Gran and Zoe, too, and even Wes. But Clayton hardly knows me, and his presence isn't giving me the comfort I seek right now.

"My phone?" I croak out.

He reaches in my back pocket and slips it out, before I can think about the fact that he briefly touched my butt. There are missed texts from Zoe and Jenny, none from Jace. But at that moment, like he knows I need him, his name flashes on the screen and it rings in my hand.

"Are you sure you should answer that right now?" Clayton asks. Is he worried what Jace will do if I tell him? Or does he think I'm too messed up to talk on the phone? I simply don't know Clayton well enough to read him.

But I answer, and the dam breaks as I relay what just happened. Tears stream down my face, and when I tell him, "Clayton saved me," I realize that Clayton has saved me so many times now, it's becoming absurd. "I don't know what would have happened if he hadn't come out when he did," I whisper.

"He should have come out sooner." Jace's growl is almost a shout and I wince, my ears ringing.

"Where are you?" he asks, his voice gentling now.

I look around. "I think I'm in a locker room."

"You're in the team locker room," Clayton tells me.

"Let me come get you, and then we need to call the police. Have you called them yet?"

"Police?" I echo. Last time shit went down with Wolfe, the police were never called. But this time, I want it to end. He needs to be in handcuffs. Why didn't we do that before?

"Can I talk to Clayton, Pep? I want to be with you and he can tell me how to get there."

I hand the phone to Clayton, trying to comprehend what all this means. The police are coming. Last time the police came, I was in Jace's dorm room, and Frankie was restraining Savannah Hawkins, who was dressed in lingerie. Why do I want Jace right now, again? All of this is because of him, isn't it? Somehow, that doesn't matter to me, and it doesn't escape me how utterly messed up that is.

A moment later, Clayton hands me back the phone and tells me Jace will be meeting us soon. Juan and Steve are suddenly there, in the room with us, dressed in jeans and with wet hair. It's so strange that I just saw them on the field.

"Nice home run," I congratulate Juan, and his eyes widen slightly before he chuckles.

"How are you feeling? You were out for a while there."

"Yeah, my head hurts," I reply lamely. My ribs and arms ache too, I'm beginning to realize.

Steve and Juan want to know what I remember about what happened, and I relay the story for a third time. By the time I'm done, Jace is there, and I'm not exactly sure how he got through security so quickly, but his face is white and his eyes wild.

When he crouches at my side and begins inspecting me with his fingers and his eyes, all his horrible mistakes go away for an instant, and I'm just grateful he's here because I suddenly feel like it's going to be okay. But then he and Clayton are exchanging tense words and they disappear, and I'm left feeling confused and exhausted. I can hear them yelling at each other and I vaguely make out that Jace wants to call the police, but Clayton doesn't. He's afraid of the publicity issue for the team. But then I hear Steve step in, and it's decided. The police will be coming. And I'll be telling them what happened, too.

When my phone rings and Zoe's name flashes, I almost answer. But I'm just so tired now, I can't bring myself to tell her what's going on. Wasn't she with Jace? Did he not tell anyone before he came here? It's not a situation I can tell halfway, and I suddenly don't have the energy to go over it again. When Jace returns to the locker room alcove where I'm resting, I finally close my eyes. Safe. For now.

Chapter Twenty-One
JACE

She stopped shaking when I placed her in my lap in the passenger seat of the minivan. Wes was driving, and Zoe, Jenny, Omar, and Rollie sat in the back seats. The rest of the crew squeezed into other cars, but we were all headed back to Brockton. The partying mentality died instantly when our friends found out what had gone down. It was solemn as hell in the minivan, but there was one unspoken message. We were all there for Pepper.

Pepper had told the cops about Wolfe and Rex, and she'd tried her best to describe the third guy, but she didn't remember much of anything about how he looked. She hadn't gotten a good look at him before he conked her on the head. Because of our run-in earlier, I'd been able to describe the guy who was with Rex and Wolfe, who I'd assumed was the same guy who attacked Pepper. Paramedics looked at her, and determined she had a concussion. She wouldn't be able to run for a few days, which she didn't like, but she was going to be okay. And when they told her someone should supervise her tonight and wake her every couple of hours, Pepper had looked at me and I'd stepped up without a second thought.

She wouldn't leave my side. It was both so crazy and so normal for her to want my comfort and protection; I was just going with it and trying not to make it mean anything too significant. But it was obvious she wanted me soothing her, and she wouldn't ask for it. So I wasn't going to think about what I deserved, and whether she was ready, and if I was overstepping my place. I was going to stay the night in her room and keep an eye on her, because whether she would say it or not, I knew I was who she needed right now, for whatever reason.

Chapter Twenty-Two

PEPPER

A sense of déjà vu washes over me when I hear the hushed voices in the kitchen the next morning. My head throbs, my body aches, and yet I sort of feel detached from my body, like none of it really happened. This is what it was like after Savannah Hawkins drugged my drink at my recruit visit to UC my senior year of high school. And the sensation that I'm watching the events of someone else's life unfold? That brings me back to the first time Wolfe and Rex tried to drag me somewhere, with an unknown purpose, nearly four years ago.

And yet, the person who caused all of it, he is the one I needed more than anyone last night. Not Clayton, who offered to let me stay at his nearby loft downtown. The guy who rescued me from first the drugging, then a hit and run, and now... whatever happened in that alley, and I didn't feel safe with him. I always thought I was a rational, reasonable person. But I'm beginning to question my own sanity.

I'm remembering that Jace slept beside me last night, though he kept a careful distance, and I simply can't deny that I wish he was still beside me. I'm not ready to face the day.

With a heavy sigh, I heave myself out of bed. But it's a mistake to glance at my reflection in the mirror, because I'm a hot mess. My hair is a tangled disaster, and my eyes are red rimmed, reminding me that I spent a good portion of the night crying. There's a scratch down my nose, presumably from my struggle with Wolfe, and bruising on my arms. Lifting my shirt, I find more purplish marks on my ribs. My chest begins to rise and fall in rapid alternation and I'm wide awake now.

I swing open my bedroom door, determined to find out if the police have any updates. They must have found him by now, or one of his friends. Jace is sitting at the table with Gran and an officer, and he quickly stands up, knocking over his chair when he sees me.

He approaches and gently pushes me back into my room, closing the door behind him. And I let him, because this self-assured Jace is one I'm familiar with, and something tells me he has my best interest in mind.

"Here, Pep, put this on." He hands me a long-sleeved shirt, and I realize I'm only wearing a thin camisole, sans bra, and sleep shorts. I do as I'm told, and he strokes my cheek lovingly, a gesture I don't fight, and even find myself leaning into.

"You stayed last night," I murmur.

"Someone had to be with you all night," he points out. He doesn't mention that I clung to him all the way from the locker room back to my bedroom. Jace hands me a glass of water that was sitting on my bedside table and I swallow a few sips.

"Do they have any news?"

"Are you ready to go out there now? It looked like you needed a minute before talking to the detective." And this time, there's a little hesitancy in his voice, like he's wondering if he was too heavy-handed earlier.

"Yeah, I want to know what's going on."

But what I find out is that there's nothing going on. They haven't found any of the three guys, or the car that Clayton, Steve and Juan described. The policeman introduces himself as Detective Marshall, and I'm unsure if that's his first or last name. He asks more questions, probing about more than just the attack, but my history with Wolfe and possible motives for his actions. Glancing at Jace, I realize I don't know how much I'm supposed to reveal. Has he already told them about the video? The previous incident? The drug-dealing? The drugs implicate Wes and Jace, and so for that reason, I keep it vague. I tell them that he sometimes crashed our high school parties years ago, and gave me a hard time.

When Jace sees where I'm going, he adds that he hung out with Wolfe a few times, but they were never good friends.

Detective Marshall doesn't seem too interested, though Gran is drilling holes through both of us.

"It doesn't sound premeditated, based on the words he said to you about spotting you at the game," Detective Marshall says. "The history is helpful, it explains that he knew you and had a reason to target you, but it's likely he's done this before with other women."

I clench the table at his words. "What do you mean?" I choke out.

Detective Marshall eyes me. "Well, it sounds to me like this assault might have turned into a sexual assault. Men who do that tend to be repeat offenders."

Even with the incident in high school, I'd refused to fully accept that was Wolfe's intention. It was too awful. "You don't think it could have been some kind of, I don't know, kidnapping type of thing? We told you about his reputation as a drug dealer and maybe even an addict."

Detective Marshall straightens his files, not making eye contact with me. "That seems less likely. It's just a good thing Clayton Dennison came out when he did." The detective glances at Jace, and he doesn't hide the question in his eyes. Why is Jace here with me, when I was meeting Clayton last night? But it's not really pertinent to his investigation, and he leaves a few minutes later.

Gran is fired up by the time the three of us are alone. "Talk. Now."

We know she doesn't mean about last night. She got all the details over the phone soon after it happened and before I even got back to the apartment. Jace shoots me a glance and I nod, letting him know I'd rather he tell the story.

When it's over, Gran says the most unexpected thing. "I don't want you seeing Clayton Dennison anymore, Pepper."

"Um, Gran? He wasn't involved with the drugs or the video or any of that stuff with Madeline and Wolfe. He's the reason I'm okay." Clayton wasn't even part of the background story we gave her. Right, so Clayton does have a different history with drugs, but that's not the point.

Jace's body is a ball of tension beside me.

"You're *not* okay." Gran's angry, maybe the angriest I've ever seen her, and she looks like she might even cry. Suddenly, I don't care that her desire for me not to see Clayton is the most absurd and random thing in light of what we've just revealed.

"Gran," I say softly. "I wasn't planning on it anyway, okay? I'm planning to call him today to tell him that."

She nods, her chin wobbling, and then she storms off to her room. Just then, the doorbell rings, and Jace goes to answer it, his body tensing once again after he looks through the peephole. But he opens it, and a huge bouquet greets me. When I see the guy standing behind it, I realize the conversation won't be over the phone after all.

"Clayton," Jace says sharply.

"Jace." Clayton's voice holds the same edge, and I suddenly realize it's up to me to intervene.

"Um, Jace?" I come up to his side and place a steadying hand on his shoulder. "I need to talk to Clayton alone, okay?"

Jace's muscles don't relax, even though he must know that I'm going to end things, if there even are 'things' to end, with Clayton, given what I just said to Gran.

Jace opens the door wider, letting Clayton inside. Both of their bodies are wired tight, and it's a relief in some ways when Jace finally leaves the apartment. The small space can only handle so much testosterone.

Clayton leans down to kiss me on the cheek, which seems a little presumptuous, but he did, after all, rescue me last night. Taking the flowers and placing them on the table, I thank him for the gesture, and then lead him to the couch.

"You really didn't have to come all the way up to Brockton on one of your rare days off, Clayton," I admonish him.

"Of course I wanted to check in on you. I'd hoped you'd stay in Denver so I could keep an eye on you last night, but I understand wanting to come home. Your Gran stayed with you, right? And checked in on you every couple hours?"

I nod, for some reason feeling it'd be inappropriate to tell him who really checked in on me. Jace had somehow changed into different clothes from last night, so he must have returned to his house. I'm glad for it. Something tells me this conversation would be harder if Clayton knew Jace had been the one taking care of me.

"I have to thank you, Clayton," I say, starting with the obvious. "You didn't hesitate to confront those guys last night, and a lot of people wouldn't have run right up to them like you did. If you hadn't been there, and reacted like you did, I can't even imagine what might have happened."

Clayton nods, accepting my thanks, and he takes my hands. "Pepper, if you hadn't been in that alley to meet me, none of this would have happened. I hope you know that I am so sorry for asking you to meet me there. There are usually other girlfriends or family too, and it didn't occur to me you'd be all alone," he adds.

I shake my head. "I don't blame you at all, Clayton, you couldn't have known. There were crowds just around the corner. It seemed safe." Well, actually, it was a little creepy, but still, it's not fair for him to blame himself. Especially when he doesn't know that Wolfe had been targeting me well before last night.

Clayton takes my hands in his then, and again I feel like he's on a different wavelength entirely about where we stand. I didn't think I'd indicated we'd progressed to this level of comfort together, but I'm so inexperienced at all this that I'm beginning to wonder if the date, the responding to texts and calls and accepting his gifts adds up to something more serious than I realized. If that's the case, it's even more important we never go on that second date I promised.

"Clayton, I just don't think we should continue trying to see each other anymore." I look up at him, wondering if I should continue with my explanation, but as usual, I find him difficult to read.

"You don't?" he asks quietly, and I wish it wasn't the case, but his voice is tinged with hurt.

"It's just, I'm about to start college again. This is a really important year for me with running, and I'm going to be so busy. And you're in the same boat with baseball," I add.

"I'd make time, Pepper. You can't tell me what I'm too busy for. I've shown you that I'll be there for you, haven't I?"

His words, once again, strike me as off. It's like we're talking about two different things. We went on one date, yet he's acting like we're in a serious relationship. Did our little flirtations in the past mean something more? Am I reading this all wrong? Man, maybe I do need to date more. I'm really clueless.

"You have Clayton, I'm sorry. I didn't mean to put words in your mouth or make assumptions about your life. The truth is, starting a relationship with you right now just isn't going to work for me." I'd mention the level of commitment it would require again, but that seems unwise at this point.

"Is this about what happened last night?"

"No," I answer immediately. But maybe it's a decent cop-out, since he's being a little bit more adamant than I expected. "Well, yeah, maybe a little. I just, it doesn't feel like the right timing," I add, hating myself for twisting the truth. I really hope I'm not giving him false hope for the future, but I'm not about to tell him I simply don't feel strongly enough about him to keep trying. He'll tell me I haven't given him a chance, and maybe he's right. But I know I'm doing the right thing. At least, it feels right. Plus, Gran told me to, and while she gives orders all the time, this one was different.

Clayton stands abruptly, and it takes me a second before I react and stand with him. He walks to the door. "I hope you feel better soon, Pepper." But he doesn't make eye contact with me, and he shuts the door hard, leaving me feeling like a total jerk.

Chapter Twenty-Three

JACE

It had been three weeks since the assault, and no sign of the attackers. I was pissed. I knew this wasn't a major crime, or at least, it didn't turn into one, in the grand scheme of things, but I was sure with enough resources, Wolfe Jenkins could be found in no time. The cops just weren't trying very hard, and it was difficult to accept that this wasn't a top priority for them, when it was constantly on my mind.

We withheld the other evidence we had against Wolfe, for now. It didn't seem to have a purpose for the moment, since the cops were already after him. If we needed it, we could bring it out, but I'd rather hold onto it. I still didn't understand why Wolfe had targeted Pepper, or what he'd had planned.

Wes left a week ago for Princeton, and we'd talked about hiring a bodyguard for Pepper. But Pepper would hate that, and she was being smart. She wasn't fighting me on driving her everywhere, and now that preseason was back up for cross country, she was never running alone. She had six housemates, and I hadn't bothered second-guessing myself when I'd sat them all down on move-in day and told them to lock the damn house, and never leave Pepper there alone. So, we'd opted against a bodyguard, and I was on edge.

At least Clayton was out of the picture. I'd watched him leave that day, knowing Bunny had probably eavesdropped on the whole conversation from her bedroom. He'd actually looked kind of upset, but he was trying to keep his cool. I could identify with that. But I hadn't felt bad for him, not really. Yeah, he'd helped Pepper out, but she wouldn't have even been in that situation in the first place if not for him, so I wasn't exactly all grateful to the guy. With the drugging incident nearly three years ago, he'd carried her out of the bar, but Ryan was there too, and he would have done it. It wasn't like Dennison was a huge hero. And with the hit and run, someone else would have come up on her momentarily if not him. I wasn't about to feel indebted to the guy.

Instead, I was waiting patiently for the right moment to tell Pepper just what I wanted from this renewed "friendship." But until I felt like there was a shot she'd trust me, really trust me, with her heart and shit, I wasn't going there. She trusted me in other ways, though, that'd become clearer with each day since the assault. But her safety was my top priority until Wolfe was behind bars.

Chapter Twenty-Four
PEPPER

We've moved into the purple house. The guys on the cross team have all lived in the same house for years, and the girls finally found one big enough for seven of us this year. It's purple. And, since the guys' team call their house "yellow house" we're going with originality too. We're hosting our first party tonight, and I'm trying to get into the spirit, but I'm wary. They haven't found Wolfe yet, and it's making it hard to relax and enjoy being back with my teammates again. I keep thinking he's going to pop out from the shadows any minute.

I'm co-captain this year with my best friend at college, Lexi Morris, and I know I've got to get my act together and focus. Though I'm only a junior, there weren't too many seniors to pick from for captain this year, and, since Lexi and I make a good team, I guess I was the choice as her co-captain. Gina Waters is the only other senior who has raced on varsity. Officially, Lexi and Gina are redshirt juniors because Lexi was out her freshman year with an injury, and Gina didn't race her junior year. Still, both are planning to graduate this spring and won't be taking advantage of their extra collegiate cross season. There are three other seniors on the team, but they've never been one of the top seven runners. Aside from Gina and Lexi, my housemates are juniors like me – Caroline Hopkins, Wren Jackson, Erin Tokac, and Kendra Smith. All of them know what happened to me this summer, and it helps to know they've got my back, but I've got to step up so Lexi doesn't have to lead the team alone.

"Girl, are you sleeping?" It's Gina, standing in my doorway and looking ready to party. She's wearing a sparkly strapless dress and has a bottle of tequila tucked under her arm.

"Is it that obvious?" I ask with a grimace. I haven't been sleeping well, not at all.

"Well, you've got some rocking raccoon eyes. Want some help with makeup?" she offers. One thing I've learned about Gina in the past year, she loves doing other people's makeup. She doesn't overdo it either, and I happily let her sit me in a chair and consult her makeup bag.

Gina left in the middle of my freshman year, not of her own volition, to get treated for bulimia and anorexia. She came back to school last fall. At first, she was so embarrassed, she'd hardly talk to any of us. Yeah, she looked different. She was a lot heavier, and she didn't like it. When her restricting and purging habits came back, she decided to quit racing for the year, because it was too hard being slower than she was when she was sick. She didn't give up on her teammates though, and I admire her for that. Instead, she got over her embarrassment and embraced us. She ran with us all the time, and eventually her muscles got used to running at a healthy weight, and her strength grew until she was right there with us at workouts.

Since preseason started last week, she's been totally confident in herself, and to say I'm relieved that she's in a good place now would be a giant understatement. I know she still struggles, but she talks about it openly.

"You rocked the hill sprints this morning," I tell her. She selects a shade of concealer and then scolds me to stop talking as she begins to apply it.

"Yeah, it's funny. When I have a good workout, I'm like, wow, imagine how fast I'd be if I weighed less! And when I have a bad workout, I think, it's because I weigh too much. But it's just that voice in my head and I try to think of it as this little devil on my shoulder who I'm supposed to brush off and ignore."

I'm about to agree with that last statement, but she shushes me again, not wanting me to mess with her work.

"Do you want me or one of us to move a mattress in here and sleep with you? Would that help?" She pulls back and then tells me I have permission to speak before rummaging around for her eye makeup.

The truth is, I'm fairly certain the only person who would help me sleep is Jace and there's no way I'm admitting that to anyone. "It's okay, I'll get over it."

"I'm going to sleep in here tonight," she announces before adding a layer of eyeshadow. "We'll see if it helps."

She ignores my protests as she admires her handiwork, and when I look in the mirror, I agree she's done a good job hiding the dark circles under my eyes. "So, are you wearing something sexy tonight, or what?"

"Why would I wear something sexy?"

"Why not? It's fun! Let's see your options." She's not real impressed when I show her a few outfits I'd normally wear to a house party. She disappears and returns with a pile of clothes, and before I know it, I'm dressed in a fire engine red bandage dress, the fabric so tight around my body it feels like a corset.

"Yeah, that one doesn't fit me anymore, but you should keep it. You need more sexy in your wardrobe."

"Yeah she does!" Lexi's voice booms from the hallway before she appears in my room.

"Dude, where have you been all day?" She was the one who had the idea for this party, and she's been totally MIA.

"With Brax," she sighs dreamily and falls dramatically on my bed. Gina and I exchange curious glances. "He's finally done it, ladies! He's declared his love for me!"

"What?!" Gina and I squeal simultaneously before bursting into giggles.

Lexi launches into a story about how he took her on a picnic after our morning workout, and told her he'd been thinking about her all summer, and decided he didn't want any more of "this back and forth shit," and she was it for him. It sounded very romantic, for a guy like Brax Hilton, who takes very little seriously. After graduating last spring, he joined the professional training group in Brockton that I'd love to be on when I graduate. Though his sponsorship deal is minimal, he's working at a local gym to make ends meet. And, apparently, he's ready to settle down with Lexi Morris.

"Well, well, well," Gina announces, holding the bottle of tequila over her head. "This calls for shots!"

It's been a long time since I've taken tequila shots, but I agree that this moment calls for a celebration. Brax and Lexi have been on and off for years, and it's about time they stop the "back and forth shit" as Brax called it.

"To love!" Lexi shouts, and Gina and I echo the sentiment before downing the liquid.

After the shot, I relent to wearing the red piece of fabric, but I put a stop to Gina trying to squeeze my feet into matching heels. I've got to go with flip-flops to tone this down. She tries chasing me around the house with red lipstick, but her own three-inch pumps slow her down. By the time our teammates arrive, I'm buzzed with energy, and feeling like a normal college girl for the first time since moving back on campus.

Surrounded by my team and in my home, I can almost relax. Yeah, I look around every once in a while, just in case Wolfe Jenkins has somehow managed to worm his way into the party, but I'm mingling, trying to spend some time with the freshmen runners and get to know them better. A few look a little shell-shocked and I wonder if this is their first real party. Or maybe they are surprised, like I was, that top college runners party so hard. They'll realize eventually that we tone it down as soon as the season picks up, but for now, I let them absorb it all.

The party grows as the night goes on, and pretty soon it's not just the cross team but the track and field team too, and plenty of faces I don't recognize. When someone snakes their arm around my shoulder, I jump involuntarily, and I'm about to shake free when the welcome smell of Jace Wilder hits me. I'm trying to hide my smile and pretend like I wasn't secretly hoping all night he'd show up. And yeah, that's probably why I let Gina convince me to wear this dress. The heat between us is instantaneous, and I haven't even made eye contact with him yet. I've taken a step back so my back is pressed to his chest, and I'd know those sculpted planes anywhere.

I've only had the one shot, but I blame it on the alcohol making me forget all the reasons he's a bad idea. My body molds to his and he sucks in a breath, moving his hand to rest on my hip. He tenses though, and for an instant, I wonder if I'm reading him all wrong. Maybe he doesn't want me again. Maybe he doesn't think the breakup was a mistake, even though, if he hasn't outright said so, he's acted like he regrets everything. But before I can pull away, he whispers in my ear, "Don't start second-guessing yourself now," and moves his hips forward, showing me that yes, he does want me.

Before I know it I'm leading him through the party and up the stairs, and suddenly, we're alone in my dark bedroom, and Jace doesn't hold back. He presses me against the wall, lifting my entire body before locking his lips on mine.

There's absolutely no stopping what's going to happen, even if I wanted to, because every touch feels inevitable. We're a tangle of limbs as he moves us to the bed, and as he does, I realize he's mumbling words of reassurance and love to me between kisses. It's not his usual style, talking through it all, but I think he wants me to know that, at least for him, this isn't just a moment of craziness, that this is something he's been hoping for and waiting for, and that begins to sink in when he joins me, until I can't think of anything at all.

Chapter Twenty-Five

JACE

"How'd you sleep?" She'd finally opened her eyes, and I was determined that she wouldn't regret what had happened last night.

I was sitting up in her bed, my confidence from last night totally out the window. Would she be angry? Upset? I had to fight the urge to wrap her in my arms; first, I had to find out where her head was at.

She rubbed her eyes and looked around the room. "Good, actually. Really good." She sounded surprised, and I couldn't help smiling with satisfaction. "I haven't really been sleeping great," she admitted with a glance in my direction. Her gaze lingered on my bare chest, but she remained a little closed off and I couldn't tell what she was thinking.

"Yeah, I found out about that in the middle of the night when Gina was trying to drag her mattress through your door," I said with a chuckle.

"Huh?" She scrunched up her face in that adorable way. "Oh," she said in realization. "Right, I forgot she wanted to try sleeping in here with me to see if it helped. I couldn't talk her out of it. Sorry."

"So, you hadn't really planned on having company last night?" The question was out before I could think it through. I wanted to explore this insomnia business, which I was angry I hadn't figured out on my own, but for now, I was not going to be a coward and avoid talking about us.

"Company? Seriously, Jace?" Shit, she was angry. She swung her legs over the bed and stood up, hands on hips. "I don't have guys over all the time, okay? Just because I went out with Clayton doesn't make me..." She threw her hands around. "Someone you don't even know. That meant something to me last night, and I thought it did to you too, and..."

I was reaching for her and tugging her down to me before she could continue. "Whoa, whoa, easy there, baby," I said, the endearment rolling off my tongue, and she melted with it. "That's not what I meant. I just wanted to talk about last night, and I was only asking if you had thought about doing something like that with me beforehand or if it was, you know, impromptu, spur of the moment, or whatever."

"Impromptu," she grumbled, apparently realizing she'd overreacted a bit. Wow, this Pepper was feisty.

"Do you want to talk about it?" I asked, trying a different approach.

"Not yet," she said quietly, and my heart sunk a little.

"Yeah, okay."

She leaned back though and tilted her head, asking for a kiss, and I happily complied. Before it could go any farther I put some space between us. "There's something I need to tell you."

Chapter Twenty-Six

PEPPER

"They found Rex," he says.

I jerk up. "What? When? Why didn't you tell me sooner?"

"Last night, and the detective will call you today; I'm not even supposed to know."

"How *do* you know?"

"I know a guy," he says with a shrug.

Right. Of course.

"What else do you know?"

"Rex was lying low, staying with a friend in Colorado Springs. He wasn't saying anything to the cops when they arrested him, and then he asked for a lawyer, so now the chances of him saying anything are even lower. I was going to tell you last night, but, um, got distracted."

"Yeah." I'm struck with sudden and acute embarrassment. Who was that girl last night? What came over me?

"Look, Pepper, I really want to talk to you about everything. Everything between us, and all the things I did."

Standing up from the bed, I walk away to my closet and throw on running clothes. "Now's not a good time, Jace." I don't elaborate, because the truth is, I've got no easily available excuse. Today is our first day off from a team workout since preseason started, which is why we had the party last night. I'm not even sure who might be up yet and if anyone will want to go on a run with me, so there's nowhere I need to be. But he doesn't pry.

"Yeah, okay. Um, do you want me to go?" What a loaded question.

Sighing, I glace over my shoulder. He looks lost. "Do you want to go on a five-mile run with me? It's a recovery day and we don't have anything scheduled." I'm surprised when he agrees, because he probably has football commitments, but ten minutes later, after he's gone home to change, we're hitting the trail by our neighborhood.

He doesn't try to talk about "us" again, which I'm grateful for, and we run in silence. I don't want to hear his apology, because it's not going to fix anything. I know what he wants to do. He wants to explain his actions from two years ago, and there are only a couple of ways that can go. One, he'll admit that he's a real asshole capable of being heartless and cruel. Even if that's the truth, I don't want to hear it. Or maybe he'll say he wasn't ready for a serious commitment, and he handled it poorly. Either way, what he's really saying is that I wasn't enough for him. And no matter what it boils down to, I don't want to rip open that wound. I've accepted it, forgiven him, and we're at a good place. If I can just avoid jumping him...

I've brought my cell with me and it rings as we're jogging back on campus. It's Detective Marshall, and he reports the same news Jace told me this morning. They found Rex, who claims he doesn't know where Wolfe is. But there's more. Rex has given a statement. He says he didn't know what Wolfe was intending to do. Wolfe asked him and the other guy, who they are hoping Rex will give more information about, to meet him by that alley with the car and help him with a "job." That's it. Rex won't say more, because clarifying what he means by "job" entails exposing more of his criminal history. Detective Marshall doesn't tell me that last part, but it's clear Rex is in a tough position. He wants to claim as small a role as possible in what happened to me, but he can't explain himself in a believable way without showing his cards.

So we're left waiting, again.

When Jace and I part ways after the run, I'm reluctant to admit that I want to ask him when I'll see him again. But I've got too much pride to let him know just how happy it makes me he's back in my life.

In lieu of a team workout, we have individual meetings with Coach Harding and the women's assistant coach, Susan. Gina's meeting was earlier in the day and as I'm leaving purple house for Coach's office, I see her coming inside. Her eyes are red and raw, and it's clear she's been crying.

"Gina, what's going on?" I try to convey patience and comfort, but I never know if I'm doing it right. Taking her in a hug, I lead her over to the couches.

"It's stupid," she says, but the tears threatening to spill over tell me a different story.

"Tell me anyway. All my problems are stupid too."

"I just had my meeting with Coach Harding and Susan," she begins. "I mean, they were perfectly nice, didn't say anything mean or whatever, it's just, they didn't really talk to me about running, or my season."

"Okay, what did they talk to you about?"

"Staying healthy. They said that my only goal should be staying healthy." Her voice trembles and I reach to take her hand, even though I'm not exactly sure why their words were so upsetting.

"You didn't expect them to say that?" I prompt.

She sighs and wipes her eyes with the back of her other hand. "No. I thought I proved myself last spring. I thought I showed everyone that I can run with the team and train with you guys without relapsing. I want, more than anything, Pepper," she says, looking me in the eye, "I want you guys to believe I'm strong. That I'm not some fragile girl who's going to snap and break. I want the coaches to treat me like a real athlete."

I swallow, unsure what to say. In some ways, I find her incredibly strong. She battled hard over the past two years to get to where she is, and she's in a good place. A lot of women would never be able to run collegiately again for physical and emotional reasons after experiencing a severe eating disorder like she did.

So that's what I tell her. "You *are* strong, Gina, and the coaches wanting your health over everything else isn't them saying otherwise.

They know how determined you are to stay healthy, and they want to support that. Maybe as the season progresses they'll talk to you more about your running goals, but you have to admit that running goals shouldn't be your priority right now." I hope I'm not screwing this up. "If doing what you love and competing helps you stay healthy, then we want you running by our side, but to keep it a healthy thing, you might not want to worry so much about your results."

She nods, but I can tell she doesn't want to hear it. Still, I think she's trying to understand. "Yeah," she says after a moment. "My times and places at workouts and meets are numbers and statistics which always make me think of the other numbers and statistics I'm not supposed to think about," she admits. "You're right, and the coaches are right too. This is about my health, not whether or not I'm in the top seven going into the Championship season."

I nod. "Right." But when we part with a hug and I make my way to the offices, I know it will be a tough season for Gina, regardless. There's joy in being part of the top seven – the varsity – with the women at UC. Pushing ourselves as a team in those final meets against some of the best in the nation, and even the world, is an indescribable feeling. It's better than individual glory, and I think in the past that's all that Gina focused on. Now she wants to experience all of it. And it's her senior year, so it's her last shot. I hope she knows that she's a part of the team whether she competes in the final meets or not, and that I'm not the only one who feels that way.

But my meeting doesn't exactly go as planned either. Coach Harding has been pretty laid-back about his goals for me in the past. He's usually vague and doesn't get down to the specifics. But this time, Coach says it straight. "It's your year to make All-American, Pepper."

That's his opener. From there, he tells me I've got a shot at the record on our home course, and a chance to win the individual title at our conference championship. I think my jaw is on the ground when he finishes.

"Why do you look so surprised?" he asks with no trace of humor.

"Well," I say after a second to recover myself. "Those are the goals I've had in my head all summer for myself, but I wasn't planning on vocalizing them."

"Why not?"

"Because I wasn't sure if they were realistic, and I didn't know if I was being stupid."

"You're not being stupid, Pepper," Susan tells me. "You've been capable of all these things since you were a freshman."

"What do you mean?" I ask, my eyes narrowing defensively.

"You haven't reached your potential," she says simply. My heart sinks. The words are hard to hear, even though I knew that would be her answer. I've known it all along.

"I know," I murmur.

"Don't be hard on yourself," Coach Harding says. "You've had some great seasons and you've been right in there on the national scene both in cross and track. Consistency as a college runner, especially for women, is definitely an important characteristic for a successful long-term running career."

"And, in terms of getting sponsorship deals later, it's more important to be consistent than to have that one awesome season and never do it again," Susan adds. She pauses, and I wonder if she's thinking of Gina, like I am. In a way, losing weight fast is a shortcut, but it comes with consequences. Hopefully if she stays healthy, she can get back on track.

"Do you think you want to run professionally after college?" Coach Harding asks.

When I say "yes" with a fervent nod, I realize I haven't told anyone this.

"You've got the talent and the personality to do it," Susan encourages me. But then we all go quiet, probably realizing we're getting ahead of ourselves. "Well, Sienna can tell you about it when the time comes. She's living it, right?"

Sienna Darling was my captain freshman year, and she's been living up in the mountains, training with her now-fiancé, who is also her coach. She recently qualified for the marathon Olympic trials.

"Right," I agree. A life of running, setting goals and chasing after them, would be a dream, and one I need to begin working toward this season.

Chapter Twenty-Seven

JACE

The girl was giving me whiplash. Emotional and mental whiplash. I didn't know what she wanted from me but I was trying damn hard to give it to her. One minute she was looking at me like she used to, like we were totally okay, and the next she was kind of cold-shouldering me, at least Pepper-style. The girl didn't really have a cold bone in her body, so her version of being standoffish was simply not being as open as she usually was. And even though she'd let me in so much farther than I'd imagined she would just a year ago, I wanted more.

The night after we'd slept together, she'd texted and asked if I wouldn't mind sleeping over for a few nights until her insomnia went away. Wouldn't mind? Was she kidding? She didn't make a move, and didn't reach for me until she was fast asleep. At least, I was pretty sure she was sound asleep when she turned over and snuggled up. And that had been the routine now for weeks. I'd come over right before she went to bed, we'd fall asleep on opposite ends of the bed, and then she'd burrow into me in the middle of the night. Aside from that, there was no other touching involved.

My roommate, Frankie, wanted to know what was going on and he thought I was being my old evasive self, when I told him I had no clue. But it was the truth. Tonight I was determined to get some dialogue going between us. My, how the roles had reversed themselves. There was a time when she'd begged me for communication, and now I knew how frustrated she must have been when I'd avoided it.

We were lying in her bed, and she'd just turned off the light.

"You know, I've never actually hooked up with anyone else since you and I first got together your junior year in high school," I said. It was an odd place to start, but if we could clear up some of the facts, maybe we could get to the rest later.

She was silent for a long time and I was worried she wasn't going to respond. "You kissed Madeline Brescoll," she said quietly.

"Yeah." My voice was hoarse from emotion. "But that was it. I knew you were watching and as soon as we were in the other room I shoved her off me. I used her."

"Used her? For what? You'd already dumped me."

Just hearing her remind me of what I'd done made me cringe. I'd *dumped* her.

"I knew you didn't think I was for real. I thought I could convince you that I meant it, that we were really over, and I didn't want you in my life, if I did something outrageous and unforgiveable. And maybe I wanted you to hate me. I thought it would help me stay away."

"It did," she stated blandly.

"Yeah, I know," I agreed.

"You weren't very subtle about it," she said quietly, but rolled over so she was looking at me. We were face to face, and my pulse quickened.

"I know. And I think you knew, all along, exactly what I was doing, didn't you?" I asked.

"No," she answered, actually laughing at the idea. "I definitely did *not* know exactly what you were doing."

"You did, though," I protested. "But that didn't make it okay. That's not what I'm saying. It's just, I know you wouldn't be able to forgive me now if you didn't understand, if you didn't know me like you do." Shit, all this time waiting to talk to her, and I was totally screwing it up. This was way harder than I'd thought. There was so much I wanted to convey to her, and I sucked at words. I was trying to get better at translating it into sentences, but it didn't come easily to me.

"Now, I do. After some time and some distance from how much you hurt me, I was able to look at it and see that you were hurting too. But no, it doesn't make it okay. Not at all. You didn't stop, Jace, you just kept on crushing me, and gave up on us, on everything. You gave up on yourself and you gave up on me, and I never want to experience that again."

I was speechless. Her words weren't unexpected, not at all, yet they robbed me of oxygen and my insides felt dry, like all the anticipation and optimism had been sucked right out of me. She sounded so resigned, having already accepted that we were done. We were over. I hadn't accepted that, and I didn't know if I could.

Chapter Twenty-Eight

PEPPER

My heart is practically galloping in an odd mixture of joy, celebration, and empathy. Jace Wilder is crying in front of me. When I draw him near, from instinct alone, and his head rests on my chest, the tears turn into sobs, and his whole body starts to convulse, like he's letting out all this despair he's been keeping inside. This turmoil inside him that's been festering for ages is leaking out, no, *pouring* out now, and it's coming in the most unexpected form. Tears, weakness, shame, but mostly *exposure*. And I'm celebrating because it's something I never ever thought I would see from Jace Wilder. It's touching me every-where, sending shoots of happiness through me because there's no denying this is exactly what he needed. What *we* needed.

He's mumbling over and over how sorry he is, and that he'll never hurt me again, but he's not perfect, he'll screw up but, oh, please, just give him another chance. It's heart-wrenching, yet I'm smiling. Grin-ning. He's a pathetic, sobbing mess, but I believe every word he's utter-ing. At least, I want to believe it so badly that I find myself soothing him, and telling him, I know, it's okay, I will give you a chance. Because aren't I? In a way, I've given him a huge chance these last couple of months.

He glances up then and breathes in deeply several times. "What?"

"I'm giving you a chance, Jace. Okay? I said I never want to experience that heartbreak from you again. I don't want you to give up on you, or me, or us, and the only way to prevent that is to never give you a chance to have anything to give up. But as soon as I let you in, just a foot in the door, you were all the way back in my life, Jace. Can't you see that? I can't stop it, even if I try. So, we'll do this thing, okay? Unless I banished you from sight, doesn't it feel a little bit inevitable?"

He smashes his mouth to mine in that instant, and my heart thuds wildly with nostalgia, love, and terror. It wants to surrender to Jace again, but I'm fighting it down, holding it back, and keeping myself from the fire. It's hot, but I'm not going to get burned this time.

———

My first cross meet of the season is a success. I get first place. Not by much, and no records, but it's my first individual collegiate cross country win. Officially, it's called a "scrimmage" because it's not part of our conference schedule, and we race teams from different divisions. It's on our home course, and I won't get another shot at the record until the conference championship, since we're hosting it.

Lexi wants to celebrate my win, but I'm not feeling it. I've been beating all my teammates at workouts, so I expected to be the top runner on our team. There weren't really any standouts on the other teams today and the win doesn't seem like a big deal. I would have been disappointed if I hadn't won, but I'm not elated that I did win. It's sort of depressing. To be honest, I think I'm just down because no one has found Wolfe yet, and it's been over a month since the attack. Detective Marshall keeps calling it an assault, but that makes me think of the other path it could have taken, which involves an additional adjective, and I do not like going there.

Finding Rex wasn't much of a help, and Detective Marshall hasn't called with an update in a while. I'm beginning to think they gave up already, and Wolfe Jenkins will be out there forever, while I'm living in fear he'll return at any moment, ready for round three. Even Clayton hasn't called recently. He continued getting in touch a few times to check up on how I'm doing, and I appreciate that. It shows he's man enough to let go of his pride at being turned down in order to follow up with my well-being. I wonder if he heard about Jace and me, but it doesn't really matter.

Jace and I are together, I guess. It's different though, really different. It's cautious, at least on my part. Jace seems to get that I want to keep this relationship at arm's length. I said it was inevitable, and that he's all the way in my life now, but that's only superficially. Yeah, he sleeps over every night, and probably will until Wolfe is found. And yeah, we talk all the time and hang out, but there isn't much showing up randomly to see each other, or unplanned romantic gestures. Jace is playing off of me, and I'm glad he gets me and knows that if he gets too carried away I won't like it.

He's probably still winding down after his game this afternoon, so I decide to head to Shadow Lane for dinner with Gran. I'm sick of cafeteria food and Lexi's threatening to drag me out to something or other after her dinner date with Brax, so it's best I get a good meal in me before she and Gina bring out the tequila bottle again.

Gran's made chicken pot pie and lemon meringue cake, two of my favorites, so I'm immediately suspicious. She's doting on me tonight and is asking me all kinds of probing questions about life instead of launching into a tale about one of her recent adventures with her BFF Lulu.

"Okay, Gran, spill," I finally interrupt after she starts inquiring about my insomnia, and whether Jace sleeping over every night helps. Do we cuddle? She wants to know. The woman's endearingly obnoxious sometimes.

Gran stretches her arms out in front of her like she's getting ready to exercise and then places her chin in her hands and gazes at me. "I'm getting married." She delivers it just like that and we stare at each other for a solid minute before I can say anything.

"To Wallace?"

"Yes! To Wallace!" she exclaims, throwing her hands up. "Who else would I marry?"

I shrug. Okay, so I thought this might happen one day, but you just never know with Gran. "When did he propose?" I ask, desperately trying to remain calm.

"Yesterday."

"Is your last name changing?" I ask.

"Heavens to Betsy, no! Bernadette Barker sounds hideous. No thank you. I've been a Jones most o' my life, and your Gramps would turn over in his grave if I gave up his name, bless him."

"Bunny Barker has a nice ring to it, don't you think?"

Gran shakes her head and points at me. "Not much is going to change, you hear, and certainly not my name."

"You're getting married, Gran," I remind her. They'll be living together. But I can't bring myself to ask where they'll be living yet. The idea that she won't be on Shadow Lane, where I've lived my entire life, is too painful. "When's the wedding?" I ask instead.

"We'll see," she says with a shrug. "We're just doing a small thing. It's the second time around for both of us, after all."

I'm helping Gran clean up and getting ready to head back to purple house when she throws me even farther off kilter.

"You know," she muses, handing me a dish to dry, "we could do a joint wedding."

"Huh? Is Lulu engaged too?" It wouldn't surprise me if they came up with some sort of scheme to get engaged and married at the same time.

"No, silly! I mean you!"

I almost drop the plate. "What?"

"You and Jace! You two will be getting married soon, maybe we could have it next summer after he graduates."

"Okay Gran, I'm leaving now," I say, hoping to brush it off and let her laugh like she didn't really mean it. But she doesn't laugh, just shoves some leftovers into a bag and sends me on my way, a devious twinkle in her eye, making me wonder if she knows me at all. Doesn't she remember what he did to me less than two years ago? Doesn't she understand that we're together because, well, because it's harder not to be? For now, that's the case, but I'll only be able to keep it this way for so long. I've just got to be able to keep my heart safe until he graduates.

For some odd reason, I find myself walking to Jace's apartment instead of purple house. I'll drop off the leftovers, and tell him about

Gran. He'll understand why I'm a little, I don't know, shaken. It's cool, I'll get through it, but changes to family dynamic are hard for me. They always have been. No one answers when I knock on the door, but it's open a crack so I decide to go in and drop off the food in their fridge. I'm leaving a sticky note on the kitchen counter when Jace's bedroom door opens, but it's not Jace who comes out.

It's Veronica Finch.

She startles and stops walking, and her expression is pure guilt. "Oh, hi Pepper," she squeaks.

"What were you doing in Jace's room?" I'm not even pretending this is a pleasant conversation. I'm ready to attack, or defend, whatever the situation calls for.

She tucks her hair behind her ear nervously. It seems a little fake, the whole guilty act, and I'm not sure why. "Oh, umm... well, Jace just left to meet you and he told me, to, um, get dressed and leave."

I stare at her. Hard. Is she messing with me?

"What? He said what you guys have isn't exclusive. You can't get mad at me," she protests, suddenly gaining confidence.

I tear past her and swing open Jace's door. I haven't been in here since he broke up with me. He still lives in the same apartment, and it's been hard for me to come back. We've been meeting at my place. I walk around, actually sniffing the air for any clues. I can't believe this is happening.

There are several framed photos of us on his dresser, and vaguely, I wonder if he just put them up, or left them there all this time. One is just of me, and it was taken this summer. I don't remember him taking it, but my head is back and I'm laughing at something. Nothing could hurt me then. And nothing can now. But then I hear Lizzie, Frankie's girlfriend, from the hallway.

"Veronica," she says angrily. "What are you doing here *this* time?"

"What do you think?" Veronica responds snobbishly.

Lizzie responds, but I can't hear her. I'm about to go out there, to find out what Lizzie meant by "this time." Has Veronica been here before? But as I'm leaving, my foot catches on something, and I glance down. It's a lacy thong. And it's not mine.

Chapter Twenty-Nine

JACE

Pepper wasn't home, but Lexi said to just wait for her because she should be home soon. Apparently Lexi wanted me to help get Pepper into party mode, since my girlfriend just won her first college meet. I was more than willing to help with that. Pepper deserved to celebrate. She'd been so focused, despite the weight on her shoulders with Wolfe still out there somewhere.

When she walked through her bedroom door and found me sitting in her armchair, scrolling through my phone, I didn't notice anything wrong at first. But then she spoke.

"So, Savannah Hawkins was too far away, huh?" She was trying for casual, but her tone was icy, something I'd never heard come from Pepper Jones.

"What?" I sat up straighter, instantly on alert.

Pepper turned slowly and looked at me. Her hands were at her sides, hanging there loosely, and I could see it was taking effort on her part. "Savannah wasn't around so you decided to go for her best friend, Veronica? She's pretty hot, I'm sure you had fun. Although, I don't know why you had to do that, *again*. This time I would have just taken your word that you wanted to end things. You didn't need to go out of your way."

"Pepper, I have absolutely no idea what you're talking about."
There was unmistakable panic in my voice, and I hoped she didn't read
it as guilt on my part. Because even though I thought I knew what she
was trying to insinuate, I was so fucking confused.

Pepper pulled out something from her pocket and held it up. It was
a lacy thong, and it was not something Pepper would wear. She was
more of a boy shorts kind of girl. I shook my head. What was
going on?

"Recognize this? It's Veronica's. I found it on the floor in your
bedroom just now, after I ran into Veronica leaving there. She said you
and I weren't exclusive. Anyway, I was dropping off leftovers from
Gran. Chicken pot pie and lemon meringue cake. It's all in your fridge
if you want it." Her haughty attitude was almost as strange and unexpected as the story she was telling me.

"Pepper," I started to defend myself. This was crazy. I wouldn't
touch Veronica with a ten-foot pole. But she wouldn't let me talk.

"Get out, Jace. And don't come back."

It was the way she said it, so final, so resolute. I followed her order.
But I looked back and told her, just so she knew, that I was innocent in
this, at least.

"Pepper. I have no idea why Veronica was at my apartment. She
must have set me up."

Pepper just slammed the door in my face.

Chapter Thirty

PEPPER

I've probably had too much to drink, but I'm actually having a great time. After Jace left, we started a dance party in the kitchen, and I never even told my housemates what happened. Honestly, it's just embarrassing at this point. The weird thing is, I'm not that upset. Actually, I'm a little relieved it happened now, when I'm still in control of myself. Tomorrow I'll probably be sad and angry, but I think this time it's different. He simply doesn't have the power to hurt me like he once did. It was actually pretty empowering slamming the door on him like I did. Maybe I have a vindictive side, after all.

We're at some house party now, I have no idea where, and most of my teammates are here. Really, I think everyone at UC is at this party. The place is gigantic and the bodies are all mashed together so tightly that I can barely move. I'm sweating and bouncing up against people, and I can't remember if I'm trying to get somewhere or if we're dancing. It's so loud in here that the voices and the music blend together with the bodies. Something spills down my neck, probably beer, and I laugh and try to spin around, but get stuck between people.

"Pepper!" It's Caroline Hopkins, and she's in my face, shouting.

"Whoa, dude! You'll break my ears in half."

She giggles. "I don't think that's what you meant."

"Where's Zeb? Isn't he visiting you this weekend?" Caroline is with our former teammate, Zebulon, who now lives in Denver. He comes up a lot though and sometimes I forget he already graduated.

"Yeah!" She's shouting again; apparently those tequila shots got to her, as well. "He's out back talking to famous dudes."

"What famous dudes? I do not like famous dudes," I tell her, as an afterthought.

"It's the Rockies guys. I heard they like to show up randomly to party in Brockton now," she says. "Probably because the pitcher likes this girl," she adds mischievously. I give her a mean face. At least I think it's a mean face, but she laughs.

"That again? Just stop." She doesn't even know that Jace is out of the picture and now I'm hearing about Dennison all over again. Grrrrrrr.

"Are you growling?" Caroline is laughing at me. Did I just growl out loud? I thought a growl but I didn't know I said it too. Maybe I should go home and put myself to bed. No, I can't do that. Because I'll be all alone at the house. And alone in my bed. Without he-who-must-not-be-named. I'm tempted to growl again.

"I need another drink," I say decidedly. If I'm not going to sleep, then I'm going the other direction. I'm weaving through people, trying to find where the drinks are, when I spot a porch that looks very inviting. It's really sticky and hot in here, and fresh air sounds wonderful. Plus, I think I see a keg.

But as I step outside, I realize the group of guys by the keg are large, athletic, and play baseball. Shoot.

"Hey! It's Pepper Jones!" Juan calls out, and five heads turn. Zeb and Ryan are talking with Clayton, Juan, and Mitch.

"You guys are at a college house party," I state, wondering if anyone else thinks this is strange.

"We wanted to come see your meet, but we had a game," Mitch tells me.

"Are you serious?"

"Yeah, remember, the guys said they would come to your home meets. There's another one though in a couple months, right?" Clayton asks. He never texted to say he was coming. I frown at him.

"No?" Juan asks, laughing at my expression.

"Yeah, Conference is home this year," I tell them, turning away to pour myself a beer. I must not do it right because it's mostly foam.

Somehow, a well of emotion stirs inside me, dark and messy. Whether it's the disappointment with the beer, the appearance of Clayton, Juan and Mitch, or simply a result of drinking too much, I'm filled with a strange sensation and I think it might be loneliness.

"I have an idea!" I proclaim, surprising myself. "I think we should do beer miles."

"Right now?" Ryan asks.

"What are beer miles?" Mitch asks.

"It's a track thing. A mile is four laps around the track, right? Well, you chug a beer between each lap and race each other. And you can't puke."

I've never participated firsthand, but plenty of my track teammates make it a tradition, and it's rarely the top milers on the team who win. Actually, keeping down four beers in a short period of time alone is hard for most people, and with the running in between, few get through the whole thing. I've been reluctant to even pretend I had a shot at completing it, but I've got a sudden urge to do something besides stand around on this porch.

"Who's with me?" I challenge.

The guys agree quickly, and I recruit Lexi, Caroline and Wren to join us. Given the intoxicated state of my housemates, and, well, myself, I'm not sure we've thought this through.

Ryan and Zeb make a run to the store to grab the right kind of beer – something light – and we meet at the outdoor track twenty minutes later. I've never been out here late at night like this and the giant empty stadium is a little intimidating. It almost feels like there are ghosts or something up there watching us as we take off our shoes. Sneakers probably would have been a smarter choice, but the beer is the hard part for me. Running faster than these baseball players will be easy.

Since all of us want to participate, we need a timer, and Ryan hooks up the giant scoreboard we sometimes use for workouts and hits the clock as we crack open the first beer. The guys kick our butts downing the first one, though Wren isn't far behind them. I'm the last one to finish, and when I finally start running, the guys are already halfway around the track, though Mitch and Juan are slowing fast, and Wren and Lexi are about to pass them. But when I finally finish the first lap, and the others are chugging the second can of beer, everything I've drunk from that night comes right back up, and there's no stopping it. The group gives me a hard time, as I'm the only one to disqualify on the first lap, but it's really out of my control. I suppose for my first time puking from drinking too much, a beer mile is the way to go.

As I cheer for the others, I vaguely wonder what to do about the puke on the grass, and if there's any way to clean it up. Mitch, the biggest one amongst us, is the next to be forced to quit, and I'm wishing we had the foresight for a trash bin. But surprisingly, the rest of the crew finishes the entire mile, though Wren and Lexi walk in the last lap. Zeb takes the win, followed by Ryan and Clayton. Zeb proclaims he's still the UC beer mile record holder, even though he didn't hit his mark tonight.

"Next time, we've got to plan for this so I can eat my pre-beer mile meal," Zeb tells us afterward.

"Which is?" I wonder.

"PB and J and definitely *not* the several beers I drank before this."

As we wander back through campus, I notice everyone is in good spirits except for Clayton, whose serious expression through the sporting event suggests he believed this was an important competition, and a bronze medal was not what he was hoping for. The more time I spend with the guy, the more he rubs me the wrong way. He needs to get over himself.

I'm feeling fairly sobered up now that I've eliminated most of the intoxicating substances from my body and it's dawning on me that at some point I'm going to have to go back to my bedroom and try to fall asleep alone for the first time in weeks. It's a depressing thought. And one I refuse to let bring me back to that emotional moment I was trying to escape.

Yellow house is the first stop, but Ryan's the only one who heads off, since Zeb doesn't live there anymore, and besides, he's staying with Caroline tonight. When we get to purple house a moment later, it's an awkward goodbye from the baseball players, because I'm not sure where they're going next, and their presence isn't exactly the norm for us on a Saturday night. We'd all agree that it was fun, but I'll be honest, if it was just Juan and Mitch, I'd have enjoyed myself more.

If Clayton thinks I'm going to say I'll call him later, or invite him to hang out tomorrow or something, he's going to be disappointed. To avoid seeing his expression, I don't look at him when we veer off the sidewalk, waving goodbyes.

When we get inside, we find Jace waiting on an armchair in the living room area by my bedroom. He watches me carefully, and when we don't greet each other like we normally would, my friends say good-night and leave us be.

"I don't want to talk, Jace," I finally tell him when they're gone. "I thought I made that clear." I'm way too sober now, and my attempts to avoid this confrontation tonight have clearly failed. Walking by him proves to be pointless, because he's up from the chair and by my side in an instant.

"Pepper, please," he pleads. "I had no idea that girl was at my apart-ment. She planted the underwear and she's going to pay for it, but please don't throw out all the progress we've made because of her."

All the progress we've made? He makes me sound like a project and that angers me. *He's* the one with issues, not me.

"I don't want to hear it, Jace," I say shortly, and try to shimmy past him into my bedroom.

He continues pleading with me, telling me he's been with no one else in years. But he's got no credibility here anymore. He ruined that a long time ago. Finally, I manage to slam the door on him, leaving him alone in the hallway, though at this point, my housemates have prob-ably heard most of it and pieced together what happened. Slamming the door wasn't as satisfying this second time around.

Once I've shut the door, I quickly flip on the lights in my room and when I look around, I realize that sleeping is not going to happen tonight. Not once Jace leaves, though he's still rambling outside my door.

I'm thinking about flinging myself on my bed and giving into the pity cry that's been threatening to spill all night, but instead I swing open my door and Jace's eyes widen.

"You can sleep on the floor. With your clothes on." Even to my own ears, I sound like a total princess. A somewhat psychotic one, at that. Because really, after finding a thong and Savannah's evil twin at her now ex-boyfriend's house, what kind of girl wants him staying in her room that night? A desperate one. As time has passed, my fear has only grown, and though I could just join Lexi in her room or something, Jace is here, right in front of me, and showing no sign that he'll be leaving anytime soon. This will solve both our problems. He has a task, and I have a bodyguard.

"I would've stayed in the hallway all night anyway," he admits when he walks through the door.

I don't answer, because the truth is, it's the window by my bed that I always picture Wolfe climbing in through; I never imagine him coming in through the front door and using the hallway to get to me.

Jace stands uncertainly in the middle of my room as I grab my sleep shorts and tee shirt before going to the bathroom to change and brush my teeth. He's sitting on my armchair when I return, but he stands up immediately, probably remembering what happened when I found him sitting there earlier today.

"I guess you can sleep in the chair."

He sits back down, but doesn't take off his shoes, and when I climb into my bed and turn off the light, I feel a little weird about the situation. Still, I'm safe; even if my former best friend and boyfriend is a lying cheat with all kinds of emotional issues, I know he'll keep me safe.

Chapter Thirty-One

JACE

After she showed me the thong and kicked me out, I gave her a couple of hours before returning. During that time, I tried to track down Veronica but she was nowhere to be found. Figures. She knew I'd be after her. My guess? The girl meant to leave the thong but wasn't planning on running into Pepper in the process. She wanted Pepper to find the underwear, but didn't want to be connected to it. I've already talked to Frankie, whose girlfriend Lizzie is on the soccer team with Veronica, and a revenge plan was set in motion. Veronica's made a lot of enemies over the years, and even her soccer teammates will be happy to see her go. I'd already suspected that she was involved to some degree with Savannah Hawkins's form of crazy, and she confirmed that for me. But knowing I would get revenge wasn't lifting my spirits as I sat in Pepper's armchair, watching her sleep.

She didn't believe me. And I couldn't think of anything I could do to change that. Even if I got Veronica to admit she was lying, Pepper would reject it. I think that Pepper wanted a reason to end what we had going on, because she was afraid of what would happen if it continued. It was easy to see, because I understood her fear. I had been there. I was just hoping she didn't have to hit rock bottom in order to break free from that fear, like I did. I had faith that she was stronger than me, and that she would figure this out without reaching that dark place I'd sent myself to.

I must have dozed for a little while, because the sound of someone coughing woke me and my eyes snapped open. It was just Pepper though, rolling over in bed. She hadn't seemed very drunk when she came home last night, but she'd smelled like she'd been drinking, and puking, and I was sure she wouldn't feel great when she woke up. But when she shuffled out of bed a few minutes later, she looked better rested than I felt.

"Do you want to go to Hal's with me for breakfast?" I asked when she came back from the bathroom. It was a long shot, I knew, but I wasn't going to back down, and she was going to realize that soon enough.

"No. I don't want to go to Hal's with you, Jace." But she didn't ask me to leave, so I sat stupidly in the chair as she skimmed her phone, raising her eyebrows at me a few times.

"You didn't take it with you last night, did you?" I asked. She must have been reading my texts for the first time, and seeing that I'd called several times.

"No. I'm not going to listen to the voicemails you left," she added.

She wasn't giving me much, and this hardened Pepper intimidated me a little. This girl who wouldn't take any shit, who slammed the door on me and then opened it a moment later, demanding I sleep on her floor, she was damn sexy.

Finally, I stood up and made my way over to her, and she fidgeted just enough to tell me she was still affected, and hadn't completely stonewalled me.

"I'm not going away, Pepper. And we're going to talk. *Really* talk, soon," I said with conviction. "Oh, and I'm coming back tonight. With an air mattress," I added before leaving, not missing the slight turn of her lips that told me she might never have believed Veronica Finch in the first place.

Chapter Thirty-Two

PEPPER

"So, what do you guys think?" I ask, after I relay what went down yesterday. It's just me, Lexi, Gina and Caroline, and we're jogging on Gina's favorite trail about a thirty-minute drive from campus. There's no one else around, and though we're all a bit hungover, it's good to get outside and stretch out after the race yesterday.

Lexi answers first. "Veronica's a bitch, Pepper, you know that. She's been scheming on ways to go after you since your freshman year."

"Yeah," Gina adds. "She and Savannah were attached at the hip, so she either shares Savannah's obsession with your boyfriend or she thinks she's avenging her or something by breaking the two of you up." I want to remind her that he's not my boyfriend anymore, but whatever.

"I wasn't around when this Savannah chick went all stalker crazy on you guys, but Veronica's definitely got a reputation and it's not a good one," Caroline adds.

"But that's my point," I protest. "You know what Jace did before. He hooked up with the ultimate mean girl from high school, in front of me. The girl had tried to break us up and everything. It's like he's so screwed up he wants to hook up with the girls who hurt us."

"Okay dude, now you're the one bringing on the drama, no

offense," Lexi tells me. "Actually, I take that back, I am trying to offend you. Because really, he didn't hook up with that girl from high school, right? He just kissed her and made you think he did?"

"So he says. And even if it's true, it doesn't make it okay!" I wasn't sure Lexi had been following all those details when I'd talked to her about it before. "Wait, are you guys on Jace's side here?" I ask, incredulous. I was sure that after I told them this, they'd go off about how they thought I was crazy for taking him back in the first place and then proceed to bash him for the rest of the year at every opportunity, and help me to keep him out of my life. But come to think of it, they never warned me, directly or indirectly, about getting back together with him.

"We're not on anyone's side," Caroline says, all calm and soothing. "But last time all that happened, he *wanted* you to think he'd been with other girls, and let you think so about that redhead."

We'd all found out later that the redhead, Melanie, had been trying to get in his pants for a while but was never successful. I'll admit, it was a huge relief at the time to know he probably hadn't cheated on me after all.

"This time," Caroline continues, "if he was still all messed up like you say, why would he bother trying to tell you it never happened?"

"Yeah," Gina agrees. "If he supposedly goes out of his way to hook up with girls who will hurt you the most, wouldn't he have flaunted it in your face or something? I mean, you found out by accident."

My jaw clenches in a final attempt not to admit that my theory about Jace is probably whack. Based on the things he's said to me and the way he's acted, it really doesn't make sense that he'd be seeing other girls this whole time. And, given his preoccupation with my safety, he wouldn't welcome a girl like Veronica Finch into his life. Still, he flipped a switch from romantic to stranger in an instant once before, and I'm not about to forget it.

I'm still trying to understand my friends' reactions when we get to the waterfall a few minutes later and climb a boulder to sit in the sun.

"You said yourself a few weeks ago that he's different, and it's easy to see for myself that he's changed," Lexi says.

"Do people really change?" I ask, not hiding my cynicism.

"Um, hello?" Gina waves her hand. "I'm a walking and talking example here." She's using a goofy voice, but I can tell she wants affirmation, and we give it to her easily.

"Dude, you are definitely not the same girl from our freshman year," Lexi says.

"Or from your sophomore year, our freshman year," Caroline adds, pointing her thumb in my direction. "You kind of scared me then," Caroline admits.

"And even last year," I add, "you still weren't comfortable in your own skin at first."

"Well, I feel different too, so that's good. All I'm saying, Pep, is that people can change and it's different this time around with you two. You're the one who's going into it carrying more hurt, and you're the one who's got more reason to be scared of the whole commitment thing than the guy in this situation."

"Commitment problems is putting it mildly, in Jace's case," I mutter.

"He doesn't seem to have commitment issues anymore," Caroline points out.

"Are you sure you aren't just trying to punish him for what he did to you before? Subconsciously, I mean," Lexi adds. "I don't actually think you'd plot that purposefully."

"Yeah," Gina jumps in before I can defend myself. "This would be a perfect opportunity to make him feel shut out and confused without an opportunity to talk to you, just like he made you feel when his mom left. Maybe your subconscious is still really pissed at him."

"You guys are relentless! Why are you so Team Jace, anyway? Besides, I'm not convinced he doesn't still have those issues, and that Veronica was for real." I'm kind of pretending to be mad and actually mad at the same time. It's confusing. I don't know what to feel anymore.

"Look, I said I was a different girl in a lot of ways, right?" Gina's still going on about this. "But it's not perfect. I've got the potential to go back to my eating disorder ways, and I still carry around the baggage from it. My body's not the same, and on bad days I want to fall back to my old habits. It's probably like that for Jace too, and it's going to be like that with your relationship."

Lexi interrupts her. "Um, Gina, are you comparing Jace's commitment issues to an eating disorder?"

"No," I say, "I think she's comparing my *relationship* with him to an eating disorder?"

How we all can laugh at these lame attempts at humor, I don't know, but it breaks the tension when we do.

"Okay, so stupid analogy," Gina admits.

"Nah, you're just saying that it's not going to magically be perfect just because he's addressed his shit and is a little different." I don't want her to feel like her words didn't get through to me, when she opened up like that. Because in a way, I totally get what she's saying. And it freaks me out, because that puts the pressure on me. I'm the one who has to accept stuff and move forward. And if I can't, then I can't have Jace.

"Yeah – I mean, for me it's worth it to not go back to the old skinny Gina. I'd rather fight it and be the new Gina."

"New Gina rocks," Lexi says, throwing an arm around her.

"I guess new Jace does too," I grumble. I'm just not sure I'm ready for him.

———

When Zoe calls later that week, she's practically bursting with happiness. Things are "off the charts" with Wes.

"What do you mean? You guys haven't seen each other in almost two months." Wes is at Princeton, playing football, and he might not even make it home until Christmas this year if the team has games during Thanksgiving.

"Yeah," she sighs. "But we Skype every night, and FaceTime, like, randomly through the day. I think I've become one of those annoying girls who is constantly on the phone with her boyfriend."

"Wait, you call him your boyfriend now?"

"Yes! And he told me he loves me, Pepper!" She's pretty much screaming and I hold the phone away from my ear for a second.

"Wow. What else did he tell you?"

"About how he used to crush on you, but like, only because you were a good friend and his only friend who was a girl, and that Jace liked you, so he thought he was supposed to like you that way too, and then when he met me he realized that his feelings were, you know, way more intense than what he felt for you, and..." she stops for a breath, "and he told me that Jace is his brother."

That part seems like an afterthought to her, like it's not earthshattering news. When I found out, I was kind of traumatized. But my history with the two of them was different.

"Were you surprised?"

"About his feelings for you? No, because Jace said something that one time, and I kind of suspected. It was actually sort of nice he cleared up that he didn't still harbor some big crush on you, because, I'm not going to lie, I've always thought he might." Yeah, that's what I thought.

"No, I mean about Jace being his brother. Jim being his dad. Wasn't that a shocker?" It's weird, for some reason I'm not as relieved that she knows about it as I thought I would be. It's like she's part of our inner circle now, and I don't know where I stand anymore. She's special to Wes in a way I never will be, and Jace and I, well, we may never be like that again either. I almost feel pushed out, like she's replacing me. But I know that's stupid, so I swallow it down and try to be happy for her. Happy that Wes trusts her with this.

"Yes and no, you know? I mean, when you found out weren't you kinda like, hot damn, I see it now. They are so totally similar, it's almost amazing no one's figured it out, right?"

"Right."

"So yeah, it's just, awesome being in love. And how's it going back with Jace? I bet the sparks are flying!"

"Uh, no." And I tell her about everything, how I'm not sure I trust him, and that even before running into Veronica things weren't like they used to be.

When Zoe reacts similarly to my housemates, and barely even entertains the idea that Jace was cheating on me, I start to detach from the conversation. Is my life so crazy that a girl scheming about hooking up with Jace is more believable than her actually hooking up with him? Is it Jace who makes my reality so twisted? Or is it me? Are my friends so accustomed to the unexpected in my life that they don't see things clearly? Or am I the one with blurred vision?

When we get off the phone some time later, I'm tempted to go on a run, even though we had a brutal workout several hours ago. Like, so tempted, I start to change into running clothes. Jace opens my door, and I head over to my computer to do homework while he sits in the armchair to do his. He's been coming over every night this week and sleeping on an air mattress. It's a pretty twisted arrangement.

But instead of taking my cue to ignore each other, he breaks the silence. "You didn't tell me Buns and Wallace are getting married."

Refusing to glance away from my laptop, I simply shrug. "Yeah, they're engaged."

"That's great. I'm so happy for Bunny, you know? She'll have someone to take care of her and to take care of as she gets older. He really loves her."

I spin in my chair and glare at him. Who does he think he is saying this lovey dovey stuff? "I can take care of her, and she takes care of me. She doesn't *need* him. That's not why they're getting married."

He keeps a steady gaze on me, and doesn't seem to react to my words.

"It's okay to need someone, Pepper. It doesn't mean she's not totally awesome on her own, but he's good for her, and it's easier doing things with someone else sometimes. They have fun together and look out for each other. Lulu's done that for her, but this is different. And you're going to be busy and some day you might have kids of your own, and this way she'll have —"

"Jace," I cut him off. "You're not being very subtle, okay? Are you trying to say I might be fine on my own but I'm better with you? Because you didn't think so two years ago," I say, turning back to my computer, and hoping I've closed the conversation. But when he shifts to the edge of the seat and opens his mouth again, I know I've done the opposite. Without meaning to, I just opened that door, and we're going there, whether I'm ready for it or not.

Chapter Thirty-Three

JACE

She wouldn't look at me, but I kept talking anyway. "Do you not believe in happily ever afters anymore? Or just not for us?" I asked.

"Just not for us," she said to the computer screen. "Let me rephrase." She tilted her head but still wouldn't make eye contact. "I'm happy. You seem happy. We will not be happy together."

"I don't believe you. And you don't believe that either. About us not being happy together. Yeah, we can be good on our own, but we're better together."

"Why are you so confident now? Where was this confidence two years ago?"

She was asking now, and I took this opportunity to tell her everything, all the things I had wanted to say starting with the day I found my mom's place empty until the day I approached her at that track cookout several months later. When I got to that part, I told her, "I knew I'd made the biggest mistake of my life at that point, but I didn't know how to fix it. And you wouldn't take me back. That's when I started seeing a counselor, or a therapist or whatever, for a few months over the summer. He helped me figure out all the stuff I just told you. Why I acted the way I did. We stopped having sessions when football started. I was busy and I think I got all I needed out of it. Mainly, I learned that I was chickenshit, a coward, just like you called it, and if I ever wanted you back I'd have to confront those fears."

"You're saying you changed for me?" she asked dubiously, and the cynicism in her voice almost stopped me. She had changed too, and it was my fault. Because some of the changes weren't good for her. Pepper had never been a distrustful, cynical person, but when it came to me, she was.

"*For* you, *because* of you, yeah, but for me too. Because that wasn't any way to live. Hell, I wasn't really living. After Annie left and I pushed you away, I was holding on by a thread, and I couldn't keep it up. I couldn't keep all my resentment and anger and whatever else inside anymore. About Annie, not you," I clarified. "It's weird, like, once I realized that it was only getting worse the more I ignored it, I started talking to my dad, and Frankie, and even Buns sometimes, about everything. And I ran too, and just let the emotions out. But you were the one every day I wanted to be talking with more than anyone. That never went away."

She was looking at me now, finally.

"How do I know you won't do it again?" she asked, barely above a whisper.

"Do what?" I thought I knew, but I needed to be sure.

"Hurt me." She meant everything: the disappearing act that day I found out Annie left, the closing her out, refusing to talk to her, breaking up with her, letting her think I had moved on.

"You have to trust me," I forced out. It was hard to say, because I didn't know if she could and if she couldn't, I didn't know where that left us. Or I did, but I didn't want to think about it.

A single tear ran down her cheek and she didn't wipe it away. "I don't know if I can."

"Do you want to?" I was in front of her now, literally on my knees, my face inches from hers.

"I don't know that either," she whispered.

More than anything, my body ached to fold her in my arms and kiss away all Pepper's confusion and doubts. But we couldn't go back to that halfway place we were at, where we gave each other our bodies but she held back the most important piece of her. So I rocked back on my heels and told her, "Okay, I'll be here, waiting."

Chapter Thirty-Four

PEPPER

It's the third meet of the season, the first official one, and the pressure's on. After the scrimmage, we had an invitational in California that we go to every year, and I won. So now I have a "winning streak" going and I almost feel like I don't deserve it, like I haven't worked hard enough for it. Yes, I go to all the workouts with the team and push myself until it hurts, but sometimes I'm only halfway present. Sometimes I feel like there's another emotion inside of me, blocking that competitive fire in me from raging with full intensity. I can't quite reach it. Whatever. I'm just making excuses. Maybe I'm just lazy and don't want to experience the physical distress that comes with giving it my all, laying it all out there on the course.

But as we gather in a circle before toeing the line, the familiar, comforting sensation that is so accurately called team *spirit* overwhelms me, and I remember that this is bigger than my own mind games. I'm part of something that's stronger than the emotions writhing around inside me. These girls want me to succeed, just like I want the same for them. Lexi offers a short pep talk and I add my three words, "Let's do this!", before we cheer and jog to the starting line.

This is the first year we've gone to this invitational. It's in

Kentucky, and instead of racing mostly west coast teams, like we did at the California invitational, this meet has teams from the east coast that we usually only see at Nationals. Jenny Mendoza is here with BU, but I only had a few minutes to chat with her during warm-up. She seems to have hit it off with her new teammates, which is no surprise, and is already one of their top runners. Hopefully we can talk more after the race.

I haven't felt nervous like this for a race in a long time. I mean, I always get pre-race jitters, but these nerves are new. Instead of pure excitement and "go get 'em" vibes, I actually have a little bit of "oh, shit, I hope I can pull this off" running through my mind when the gun goes off. In an odd way, it's refreshing. All that optimism seems false, because as soon as I reach a steep hill or see the finish line, my body trembles in fear, unable to bring it up to the next level, and settling for a more comfortable pace. To be clear, racing is never comfortable, but there are levels of pain, and I know I'm not reaching the black zone – that place where you actually kind of black out from the pain, but you are so proud of yourself afterward. I'm more in the purple zone – the same pangs I get at practice, hazy twinges that make me feel good about myself for working hard but are totally manageable.

It's almost like I've become complacent, and as soon as I hit a certain level of pain, when it becomes hard, I back off and say, "Enough." That didn't used to be me. I used to work through it, but somewhere along the way, I got scared. Jace might have been right about one thing. It's fear holding me back. Fear that I'm not good enough? Fear that I'll fail even if I give it my all? I'm not really sure.

I'm overthinking everything as I stride along with the other runners through the first mile. Is this pace right? Does it hurt too much or not enough? Should I break away now or later? Wait, I'm not even with the front runners here, I suddenly realize, as Coach Harding shouts for me pick it up. What am I doing? I surge forward, passing girls as I look ahead to where the leaders roll through the two-mile marker.

I'm slightly panicked, but not because I don't think I can catch them; if anything, I do well when I come from behind, especially if it's not the very end of the race and I've got a couple miles to go. No, I'm freaking out because I completely spaced out the first half of the race. That might be a first. Well, I was thinking, but not in the moment. Shit, I'm doing it again.

Get the girl in the purple uniform first, then the yellow one, then hang on with the one in baby blue. She looks like she's got a great pace going, and I should follow her until mile three, then go for it. I start talking myself through the actual people in front of me instead of getting carried away with introspection. Now is not the time for that.

And for next mile, I'm having fun, enjoying the thrill of chasing someone and catching them and then doing it again. I've been with the girl in baby blue, from the University of North Carolina, I think, for a couple of minutes, and I can see mile marker three ahead. There's a group of five ahead of us, the lead pack, and I've been contemplating when to go after them. But my body is definitely in the purple zone already, with edges of black, and if I push forward now, I might bonk before the finish line. College cross courses are 6K, or 3.7 miles, and it's easy to forget it when I see the three-mile marker. In high school, races were only 5K, or 3.1 miles, and that last marker meant the end of the race, finish line in sight.

So I settle in behind the girl in baby blue, and when the finish line finally does come in sight, the lead pack is too far for me to reach. A couple of girls try to sprint past me, and I dig a little deeper in order to fend them off, coming in ahead of baby blue and the others and feeling like I didn't give up entirely. But I know I did give up, early on in the race, when I chose not to go with the leaders. I should have been with them, but didn't want to test myself.

Sixth place is a really respectable finish at a big invitational like this one, but I find myself struggling to put on a happy front for my team when I chat with Jenny after the race and when the team stops at the Olive Garden for dinner before catching a late flight home. I'm angry with myself. Why didn't I just go for the win? I talked myself out of it before it even got tough.

After the race, Jenny gave me the nitty-gritty on the non-running aspects of her life, like Rollie. He's been incredible supportive, and they're finding a new groove in Boston, adjusting to a relationship in the midst of the college social scene and academic demands. A tiny part of me is jealous that the transition is going so smoothly for her, even though I'm relieved and happy the two of them are still going strong. I know better than anyone how hard change can be on relationships. Somehow, hearing about how great things are going with my friends' relationships – Zoe and Wes, Lexi and Brax, Jenny and Rollie – it fuels a fire in me, and not a good one. Loneliness, regret, betrayal, it all rears its ugly head when I think of what could have been for me and Jace. But maybe I'm just in a bad mood from the race; just like everything seems wonderful after a good race, everything seems uglier after a bad race. Jenny wisely didn't probe me about Jace, and I was thankful for that.

Caroline's beside me on the flight home, and when we're in the air, she calls me out on my fake happy act.

"You're bummed about the race," she says quietly.

"Not really, it was fine," I respond vaguely. I hate this feeling, being upset about my race when I beat my friends and teammates. I've gotten over it a bit so it doesn't feel awkward, but I still feel kind of self-indulgent. I should be happy I've got the talent to run so fast, right? But that's the thing, I know I've got a gift, and I want to do it justice, nurture it and develop it like I should.

"Come on, you suck at faking it, Pepper. I know you're mad about something. What is it?" There are a lot of ways I could avoid answering truthfully; I could pretend it was Jace, or Wolfe, or Gran's engagement. But I've been shying away from honest conversations a lot lately, especially with Jace, and I've got to let some of this turmoil out into the light.

So I tell her everything, all the thoughts that run through my head when I'm racing, the reluctance to test myself, the inability to break through that barrier and push through to the next level. It feels good, sharing this with Caroline. She's always been a good listener; she doesn't interrupt, but her facial expressions tell me she's listening intently. And she rarely gives advice, so when she does, I listen.

"Are you angry about something else? Something that might not have anything to do with running?" She doesn't ask this like a psychologist might, like she knows the right answer, and wants me to say it.

Actually, she asks it likes she's reflecting on something totally unrelated to me and my issues.

"What do you mean?"

"It's just, everything you said, it sounds a lot like how I felt after my dad died."

Instantly, I feel terrible. Caroline doesn't talk a lot about her dad, but I know he died of cancer the summer before her sophomore year in high school.

"After he died, I lost a lot of weight, which I think I've mentioned before. I started running really fast, and the times I ran that cross season are probably the reason I got recruited to UC," she admits. "But I couldn't maintain it without injury and I missed track season. I came back for cross season junior year in good shape and at a healthy weight, but I guess I went through what you're describing. I just couldn't get to that intense level I was seeking, the one where you know, without a doubt, there's nothing left in your system to give. That's the best feeling, you know? Because no matter what place you get or what your time is, you feel awesome about the race."

"Yeah," I breathe out. She totally gets it. And just knowing that eases some of my regret from the race today. "So, what happened? Do you still feel like that?"

"No," she replies with conviction. "Sure, I have an occasional day like that, but it's rare."

"What changed?" Tell me! Fix me!

She offers a weak smile. "Not to discourage you, but for me, it took time. I saw a counselor for years after my dad died. Actually, I saw one through my freshman year of college. And I realized I was really angry. Have you heard of the five stages of grief?" I nod. "I guess I got stuck on anger. And I got stuck because there wasn't anyone logical to direct the anger at, besides God, and so it just kind of festered. But over time, the grief got easier and easier, and I think it was really once I got to college that I began to move on and accept it and let go of the anger."

"Really?" I'm intrigued, fascinated really. I've forgotten all about my own inner turmoil as I think back to Caroline freshman year. She was so quiet most of time, and then occasionally she'd voice an opinion, and it always seemed profound, like she'd really been paying attention. Now she voices her opinions freely, though with more reserve than Gina or Lexi. I knew, of course I knew, that her father dying when she was fifteen was hard on her and affected her, but she'd never shared how it affected her running.

"Yeah, I mean, I think the biggest turning point for me was when I realized what it was that I was feeling. I didn't express anger like most teenage girls, I guess," she says with a little laugh. "I didn't do anything rebellious, I just kind of shut down, shut people out. My senior year of high school, I realized I didn't have many friends, and I pretty much never did anything fun. I was still into running, but I knew I didn't have that same competitive nature I used to have. The one that got me hooked in the first place."

Caroline's speaking passionately but quietly. By the way she's wringing her hands, I can tell this isn't something she's repeated many times. It's still raw for her. And maybe that's why she saw through my act, and identifies with me. She takes a deep breath before continuing.

"I was starting to realize it was anger about what happened to my dad, and that I needed to let myself feel that and go through it, when I started college. Just knowing what it was that was making it hard for me to have good friendships and race like I used to, that made a big difference. But then when I started here, I don't know, all you guys, my new teammates and roommates, it like, jumpstarted something inside me, got me to move past my anger. It's really hard to explain. But when you see people who love racing and love their teammates, and experience so much joy from the same things as me, it makes it harder to be angry at God or what happened to me."

I rest my head on her shoulder then, letting her story seep into me and latch on to my own story. Her way of grieving has similarities to my own, but of course, I find myself thinking of Jace, and how he's dealt with grief over the years. Not just when he broke up with me, but before Annie even returned. I wonder if now he's finally moving on. If something jumpstarted it for him. Or someone.

Chapter Thirty-Five

JACE

"Hey, man, I'm headed out," I said as I thumped Frankie on the shoulder.

"It's early, Jace, hang out for a while," he said. It was poker night at our place, but I didn't join the card game tonight. We usually have Saturday football games, so when we're not traveling, we keep ourselves in check by meeting up for cards on Friday nights. I figured most college football players always had the usual temptations of women and partying, but it seemed that ever since our team started winning again, the invitations and pressure to be the life of the party got a little out of control. As co-captains, Frankie and I have tried to set a good example.

"Not tonight, Frankie. Pepper's got her conference meet tomorrow morning. She's going to bed early." I've continued coming over, sleeping on an air mattress in her room. The fear that Wolfe would pull a crazy on her was still there, and even though I wanted it gone, I loved having an excuse to see her every night.

At that point, the rest of my teammates knew I stayed at purple house every night, and they thought we were together again, an assumption I was not going to correct. As I left, a few called out to tell her good luck.

She hadn't pushed me away yet, even if she hadn't pulled me in either. I was letting her see that I was the same Jace she'd been friends with forever, and that she could trust me like she used to. But I was also trying to show her that I was different too, that I wasn't going to shut down on her and let her down. I was confiding in her about all the things I was feeling, the good and the bad. I could almost see the little wheels in her head turning. It's like Buns said, the girl thought everything through. And I wanted her to, if that's what it took, because I was counting on her to eventually conclude I was good for her. The more time I spent with her, the more I believed it myself.

Chapter Thirty-Six

PEPPER

The Conference meet comes before I'm ready for it. It's already November, and assuming I qualify for Nationals, I've only got three more meets this season, two if I don't qualify. Conference, Regionals, and Nationals. Today I have a chance to do something awesome. The course rotates every year for Conference, and we won't be hosting again for another seven years. If everything comes together I could win *and* set a course record on our home course.

My body is in amazing shape. I can feel it with every workout. Physically, I'm a finely-tuned machine. If I can just find it in myself to dig deep and stop self-doubting enough to break through to the next level, my body will follow. I've thought a little about what Caroline said on the plane – that anger and grief prevented her from embracing her competitive nature. But I haven't experienced anything like she did. All I can think is that I'm really angry at Jace, and maybe it goes back even farther than when he broke up with me. Maybe I'm mad at him for all the years he "grieved" his mother's abandonment by sleeping around and partying. I don't know. It seems like old history now, it's hard to imagine I'm still hung up on it.

Yet the more I've thought about it, the more it resonates. I think that's what I latched on to about Veronica's lie. Because deep down, I knew right away it was a lie, even before Jace denied it, and my friends weighed in. I just wanted a reason to be able to express this anger that, apparently, I've been burying. Still, I'm doubtful that the admission or acknowledgement that, yeah, I had some anger in there about Jace still lingering, will translate to racing harder.

When the gun goes off and I surge forward with bodies pressed close to me, I hope that I can beat down my fear today. Because I think that more than anger or anything else, it's fear that's holding me back. Bunny, Wallace, Lulu, Jim and Jace have come to cheer me on, and as I settle into the lead pack, their voices ring in my ears. Gina's voice comes through, too. She wasn't one of the top seven this year, but she was close. She's the alternate for the Championship season, which means if any of us get sick or injured, she'll race. It also means she comes to all the workouts still and will travel with the team to Regionals and Nationals. She's been handling it well so far.

It's one of those perfect race days. Brisk, but not cold. I'm confident in my stride and pace as we pass through the second mile on a trail I've run hundreds of times. It's one of those races that almost feels easy, and everything about it is familiar, almost nostalgic in an odd way. But no matter how many races I've run or won, it doesn't diminish the importance of this one. I want to win *this* meet on *this* course more than anything in this moment, and when we hit a cluster of trees that signifies a half mile left to the finish, I pick up the pace, trying to pull away from the pack. But there's a runner at my side, Whitney Simmons, a senior who placed second at Conference last year. I had a feeling she'd be going for the win today, too. She probably wants it as much as I do, and I relish the challenge, because it means we'll run faster together, and I may get that record too.

But when the finish line comes into sight, my body begins to stall. It's hurting, like it always does at this point, and I'm not sure I've got what it takes to beat this girl. I hear my friends and family shouting my name and with their enthusiasm I'm reminded of my purpose here. The sensation I had when I came here over the summer, the need to win when it matters, to see just how fast I can be, it pulses through me. Whitney beside me begins to pull away, and my legs and chest scream at the idea of following her. But I'm going to ignore the self-doubt, and try anyway. Even if I don't have what it takes to beat this girl, I've got to see what I *do* have, and I'm not going to back off and hand it to her. Despite its initial protest, my body knows just what I'm asking it do when I open my stride and let loose.

It's freeing, sprinting with abandon like this. I'm not listening to any of the pain signals telling me it's too much, that it hurts, that I'm not strong enough to reach the finish line first. I'm completely cut off from all that negativity and my arms pump with the liberating sensation of going full tilt, no holding back. It's like my competitive spirit came out of hiding, and she is fiercely reestablishing her place in my body.

I'm on my own when I burst through the tape, hands in the air. And I didn't miss the clock highlighting my time as I pulled away from my competition. The course record has been shattered.

———

It's been a long time since I've floated on this kind of post-win bliss. My cheeks are starting to hurt because I just can't stop smiling. That, and everyone wants photos. We took the team title too, so I'm not the only one coasting from the euphoria that can only be found after an awesome cross race. The best part? Gina Waters seems happier today than she was when she won this race two years ago. I think she had her own breakthrough out there, cheering for us along the course. She was the first to congratulate me and I'm pretty sure she had happy tears in her eyes when she pummeled me with a full-body tackle hug.

The only thing missing is Jace. Right, person... the only *person* missing is Jace. Sometimes he seems more like a phenomenon than an actual living breathing dude. His presence is that all-consuming for me. I haven't said any of this to him lately though, and I'm beginning to think that's been a mistake. What have I been waiting for, anyway? It's almost like I experienced an epiphany today, and I want to share it with him. It's that pushing through the pain is worth it, even if you risk getting burned. It's not all that profound, not really, but I think it worked for me on the course today and I'm willing to try the same approach with Jace. That second where I just said, to hell with hurting and self-doubt and the chance I'll lose anyway, that was the hard part. After that, it felt good to sprint. So yeah, maybe I'm just experiencing that weird state where I'm almost drunk with happiness after a race, but I'm totally wishing Jace was here so I could relay my insight.

I think he just might understand, too.

But Jim told me Jace had to run off to something, and he left a note saying congratulations and that he knew I was going to win. We don't have each other's schedules memorized anymore, but I'm not surprised he had to head out. I don't think his game starts until seven tonight, but maybe the team had meetings beforehand. It seems like the football team is constantly watching footage and talking strategy. I guess I'll just have to wait until later tonight, after his game.

It's still only noon by the time they finish the award ceremony, and it's strange to have the whole day ahead of me after a race, when usually we have to travel. After showering and changing in the locker rooms, we head over to Chapman Hall, which is open for all the visiting cross teams too.

"Did you see Clayton Dennison at the race?" Gina asks when we've loaded our trays and sat down.

"No, why? Was he there?" They did say they might come, and the Rockies' season is over, so he might be visiting Brockton again.

"I don't know. I might have seen him at the beginning of the race, but probably not."

"Doubt it. We don't really keep in touch anymore."

"You did beer miles with him, what, like, a month ago," she reminds me. "That had to be a bonding experience, right?"

"Not really." That was the last time any of us drank for the rest of the season, and our weekends have been quite a bit tamer since then, consisting mostly of couch time between workouts. I don't want to think about Clayton or that night and what led to my uncharacteristic drinking, and Gina seems to get the hint. I'm more in the mood to think about the here and now, and the future. With two more big meets, and a newfound confidence, I'm feeling unstoppable. Not to mention, Jace said he'd be waiting, and I'm ready to let him know the waiting is over.

We head back to purple house to decompress before rallying again to go to the football game. I'm not always around to watch, but I'm glad I can come to this one because it's the last one in the regular season before playoffs. I'm too energized from the race and filled with anticipation to see Jace later tonight, and I can't pay attention to the TV show my housemates are watching. Instead, I clean my room and start a load of laundry before deciding to make a quick trip to the mini-mart to restock my snack stash.

"You guys want anything?" I ask everyone before heading out, but I just get a few absent mumblings because half of them are dozing and the other half are immersed in the show.

My basket's full of popcorn and pretzels when I get in line at the checkout and find Clayton Dennison is in front of me.

"Hey, Clayton."

He turns around, and his face lights up when he sees me. "Hi, Pepper! Great race. Congrats." He leans in for a short hug, and I realize that, despite some weirdness, he's become someone I can call a friend.

"Were you at the race?"

"Yeah, but I had to head out right after watching you finish, so I didn't get a chance to say hi."

"Oh, cool. Well, thanks for coming."

We finish checking out, and he turns to me on the sidewalk. "It's a pretty good day, huh? You win the race, break a record, and then you get the call that they found Wolfe Jenkins."

"Wait. What? They found Wolfe?"

Clayton frowns, apparently confused that he's the one breaking this news. "I thought they usually informed the victim before everyone else."

"Yeah, they told me they'd call as soon as they had any news." I'm already checking my phone, making sure I didn't miss anything. Jace called half an hour ago, but didn't leave a message. It's the only call I've missed.

"That's weird. Maybe they knew you had a meet or something. Who knows? But yeah, they arrested him this morning."

"What's he saying? Where was he?" The fear I've been carrying for over two months now falls away so abruptly with this news that I feel weightless. But I want answers.

"Here, I'll give you a ride back to your place and fill you in," he offers, taking my grocery bag. I'd rather he just tell me right here and then I can call Detective Marshall myself, and then tell Gran, and Jace, and my housemates. Man, do I have a lot to celebrate tonight, or what? But I don't want to offend Clayton, so I get into the passenger seat of his car.

"Hey, do you mind if we swing by the Marriott? I got this stuff for the guys and then maybe we can grab a bite to eat or something and catch up."

"Um, I think my housemates already ordered pizza for an early dinner tonight," I lie. Is he seriously trying to get me to go out with him again? "So, Wolfe?" I attempt to get him back on track before he gets ahead of himself.

"Right. You know, the guys are going to want to hear all this and say hi to you, so why don't we just go over all of it together, yeah?"

"You mean, at the hotel? Why are they in Brockton, anyway?" I'm trying not to sound judgmental about it, but I'm just not sure why they keep coming back.

Clayton doesn't seem to mind my question. "We spend a lot of time in Denver, and it's nice to get away sometimes. They've had fun the last couple times they came up here, so when I said I'd be heading home for a few weeks after the season, a few guys decided to come up for the weekend. It's just Mitch, Juan and Steve. They're the only ones who really know about what went down with you and Wolfe. They keep asking about it. They're worried about you. I just found out on my way over to the store, so I haven't had a chance to tell them yet."

"They were at the meet too?" Surely, a group of Rockies players would have attracted attention and I would have heard about it.

Clayton hesitates. "No, they didn't get here on time. Those guys suck at waking up early for anything that's not a required practice."

I realize we're already at the Marriott, and I'm about to text my housemates to let them know I'll be a little longer than originally planned, but I'm not in the mood to tell them about Clayton and his crew being back in town. Besides, they were all totally spaced out and probably won't even notice. This shouldn't take long. I'm anxious to hear about Wolfe's arrest and what Clayton knows, and it must be quite the story if he couldn't just tell me in the car.

But when we get off the elevator and Clayton slides his card to open the door, I find that we're the only ones in the hotel room, and Clayton doesn't seem at all surprised by this fact. Actually, he looks quite pleased with himself. The fear I'd just shed moments earlier seeps back into me, and it's so heavy this time I feel glued in place, unable to move from where I'm standing in the hotel room entry.

"Sit down, Pepper," Clayton commands. "I've got a story to tell you."

Chapter Thirty-Seven

JACE

The call came when Pepper was warming up for her race. It was Wolfe, and he wanted to meet. He was trying to sound controlled and confident but there was a note of fear underneath it, one I wouldn't have detected if I wasn't so intimate with the emotion myself. When I asked what he wanted, he only said that he had information for me and he was planning on turning himself in if we could come to an agreement.

I took the address and as soon as my girl crossed the finish line, I was on the road. I called Frankie to tell him where I was going, and he insisted on joining me. I picked him up from Lizzie's place and we made it to the Denver address in record time. It was a duplex in a decent neighborhood, and Wolfe opened the door as we approached.

He eyed Frankie for a long time, asked if he was a cop, and then let us inside. I'd thought about calling my cop friend, but had decided against it. Some things are better handled without law enforcement, and I had a feeling this might be one of those things. The place was clean and sparsely decorated. As far as I could tell, no one else was around.

The conversation began with a strange negotiation. I didn't really know what we were negotiating at first and we were dancing around each other. "I've got important information," he kept saying, "and in return, I want your girl to drop the charges."

"First of all," I told him, "Pepper isn't a prosecutor. She doesn't decide whether to press charges."

"She can drop her testimony or statement or whatever," Wolfe urged.

It was a pointless back and forth, and what was he going to do, take my word for it? Besides, I would never agree to anything without Pepper's consent. In the end, I told him it depended on what he had to tell me. "If I bring everything I have against you, you're going to be put away for a long time. If I don't, you might be able to work a decent deal on what you most recently pulled. It really depends on what you've got to tell me."

See, somehow Wolfe had managed to keep a clean record. He liked to intimidate and scare people, but my gut had always told me he was not as dangerous as he seemed. I had spent some time with the guy in the past, and he was irresponsible and unpredictable, but he didn't seem capable of the kind of shit he had pulled with Pepper. I had always thought he was just trying to scare her and get to me with the first incident at the pool house. If I had suspected he was going to do worse, I would've dealt with him differently. Now, with the recent attack, I'd wondered if he'd changed. If he'd done too many drugs, or if I'd misunderstood him from the beginning. But here in this house, seeing what months of hiding had done to the guy, I could tell he was resigned to doing time, but he wanted to minimize it. And now I was curious as hell as to why he did what he did.

And when he finally told me, I realized that it had been right in front of me. It was like he was telling me what I already knew, I just hadn't put it together.

"It was a lot of money, and I really needed it. I owed some bad guys and she wasn't supposed to get knocked out, man," he was saying. "My buddy got freaked out or something, I don't know why he did that." He was making excuses but I was tuning him out now.

Immediately, I called Pepper, and when she didn't answer, a deep sense of foreboding sent me out the door and into my Jeep, with Wolfe calling out behind me and Frankie jogging to get in the passenger seat. I'm not sure why it felt like now that I knew, Pepper was suddenly in more danger than before Wolfe told me. It wasn't logical, but as we drove back to Brockton at top speed, I felt like I was racing a clock, and that time was not on my side.

Chapter Thirty-Eight

PEPPER

"Clayton?" I ask, uncertainly. "I thought you said some of your friends were here. Where are Juan, Mitch and Steve?"

"They aren't here, Pepper. I lied."

I take a deep breath and force myself to look at him. "What's going on?" He's blocking the door, and only inches from me, and there's nowhere for me to go.

He deadbolts the door and says again, "Sit, and I'll explain everything." When he walks toward me, crowding me in, I've got no choice but to back up until I hit the bed, and sit down. He leans back against the dresser, a couple of feet away, and crosses his arms. My eyes dart to the door and Clayton stiffens. "I'm not against tying you up and gagging you if you try anything, Pepper."

And that's when I know this is real. My chest squeezes, and a million disjointed thoughts race through my brain. I'm trying to remember everything through a new lens, trying not to think about what Clayton is planning next, and desperately trying to be smart and figure out how I can get out of this situation. No one knows where I am. No one even knows to look for me. And worse, I'm beginning to realize that in all likelihood, no one knows Clayton is dangerous. If anyone saw us come in here, they wouldn't think it was odd.

"I've waited for you for seven years, did you know that?" he asks.

I shake my head, and a strange, surreal calmness washes over me as I realize he wants to tell me every detail, and if I can get him talking for long enough, maybe someone will find me. Okay, I doubt anyone will find me, but maybe, just maybe, something will happen that will get me out of this. Or maybe all he wants to do is talk.

"I saw you for the first time at a cross country practice your freshman year when I was leaving school. I didn't know who you were, then, but I found out easily enough. Everyone said you were Jace's girl, but that's not why I noticed you. You've always thought it was because of him, but it wasn't. This has nothing to do with Jace." It's strange, he sounds almost normal. Not delusional at all. If he hadn't said something about tying me up, I'd wonder if I was totally misunderstanding what was going on here.

"But he's always been a problem," Clayton says with a sigh. "I knew it was a reach when I asked you to prom. You were too young, then. And I put my feelings for you aside for a long time. But by the time you were old enough, you were with Jace."

He stands up then and opens the mini-bar fridge to remove a water. After unscrewing the cap he takes a long sip and then offers it to me. Though my throat is dry as sandpaper, I shake my head.

"Savannah Hawkins was into me then, but she'd always had a thing for Wilder. I saw that she wanted him almost as much as I wanted you, and we worked together to pull you two apart. She went off-script though, and got carried away. I was supposed to look like the hero in all of it, but you just ran right back to Jace. Why did you do that?"

He watches me, and he's so controlled, it almost feels like we're having an ordinary conversation. I shrug, not wanting to shake him up. "We've known each other a long time." It's a stupid explanation, but I'm suddenly all too aware that each word I utter matters to Clayton.

"Well, it was a mistake," he snaps. "You considered me a few times, I know you did. That night, when we danced together? That was when I knew it was going to happen for us." He's jumped to my freshman year of college, when Annie left and Jace broke up with me. "I couldn't believe it when Jace just dumped you like that. He didn't know what he was losing, did he?" Clayton moves forward now, and when he places his finger underneath my chin and raises it so I'm forced to look at him, I don't flinch.

"You weren't interested in anyone after that, and the timing was off, which is why I waited until this summer. I'm the pitcher on a major league team, I've got my own money, and you were ready to start seeing someone again. You've always liked me, haven't you?" he asks, a twinge of insecurity in his tone.

"Yes," I say immediately.

He smirks. "I know. But then Wilder came back at the same time, and I had to change my strategy. Saving you from Wolfe didn't help my cause like it was supposed to, not at all." He's frowning now, and I try to hide my gasp. He set that up, too. I'd been too immersed with his revelation about working with Savannah to think about the most recent events. "It scared you off, instead. And right into Wilder's arms."

My stomach churns and I'm beginning to feel light-headed. The calmness that held me for the past few minutes is disappearing quickly because his story is almost done now, and then what?

"You weren't supposed to see Veronica Finch, she was only meant to plant some evidence here and there, but that run-in worked perfectly, didn't it? When I came to campus that night to see you though, you didn't react like I expected."

"What do you mean?" I ask. We'd hung out, hadn't we?

He moves to sit on the bed beside me and I try not to react but my body stiffens involuntarily. "You should have seen what was right in front of you. Don't you think?" he asks darkly, tilting his head and leaning forward.

"You?" I whisper, because my vocal chords won't work properly.

He nods. "My teammates were there, and they like you, you like them. It was an easy way to make the whole thing feel more natural. But you just didn't get it." His voice rises in anger, just a little, but enough to make me want to dash for the door. I know it won't do any good so I attempt to remain still.

"I was beginning to wonder if you'd ever see me the way I wanted you to. And I came alone today, to watch your meet, hopeful that this might be the turning point for us. Jace was there too, and he darted off as soon as you finished. A few minutes later, I got a call that Jace was on his way to talk to Wolfe, who was going to turn himself in."

My fists clench into the bedspread as I try desperately not to let my face reveal my shock. Was Wolfe found after all? Why would Jace visit him in jail before telling me?

"Who called you?" I ask. Why was Clayton called before I was?

"A guy who owes me. He was the one who hit you on the head, which was not something I wanted, by the way. He's friends with Wolfe, and the cops don't know who he is yet. Wolfe told him they should turn themselves in, and that he wanted to talk to Wilder before he did. Either Wolfe has some connection to Wilder I don't know about, or I pegged Wolfe wrong, and the guy is feeling remorseful. Either way, I knew Wolfe was going to tell him that I paid him to drag you away after the game. Wolfe doesn't know the rest, but Jace probably figured it out. He's not stupid. I'm only surprised Wilder didn't suspect me earlier," Clayton muses.

So Wolfe hasn't been arrested yet. And he probably wanted to talk to Jace about the evidence he has from the Madeline Brescoll debacle.

"I came straight to you after that. Pepper," he says, his voice suddenly gentle, and when he moves to touch my cheek, it takes all my willpower to stay in place. "I've waited a long time for this, and I'm not going to wait any longer."

"For this?" I'm shaking, and there's no stopping it. "What do you mean?"

"What do you think I mean?" he says, and he moves so close, our legs are pressed to each other. But apparently he's a patient guy, because aside from my face, he hasn't touched me yet.

"Clayton, if we leave now, we can explain everything together. It looks really bad, all that you've told me, but I'll help cover for you, and we can move on." I have no idea what I'm saying, what lies I'm spewing, but they come out anyway, as I scoot just a few inches away. He notices.

"I don't believe you. And it's not a risk I'm willing to take."

Chapter Thirty-Nine
JACE

I went straight to purple house first, and Pepper's housemates didn't seem worried. "She went to the mini-mart," Wren told me.

"How long ago?" I asked. The girls on the couch looked between me and Frankie uncertainly.

"Maybe half an hour, she should be back any minute," Wren said, unconcerned.

Lexi added, "She was walking, so I think she was only getting a couple things."

"Have you guys seen Clayton Dennison today?" Frankie asked, getting to the point.

The girls seemed more alert now, sensing that this might be important. I hadn't decided yet. She might walk in that door any second, and then we could handle everything together.

The girls knew who Clayton was but they shook their heads no, until Gina said, "He might have been at the race this morning. I thought I saw him for a second but I'm not sure."

"If you see him, call me immediately, okay?" I asked them.

"Is something wrong? Should we be worried?" Lexi asked.

I glanced at Frankie, who was not hiding his emotions very well. He was tense as hell. "Yeah, but we've just got to find her, and we'll explain later," I said, realizing that the girls were bound to have a ton of questions, and I couldn't spend time answering them. I just had a feeling that Pepper needed me right now, and when we left, I told Frankie to call the cops while I kept looking for her. She wasn't at the mini-mart, or Shadow Lane either, or my apartment, and there really weren't any other places she could be. Next, I went to Clayton's parents' house, but his mom said he wasn't home. As far as she knew, he was still in Denver.

I was driving around town now, my panic mounting, when I got a phone call from a number I didn't recognize.

"Hello?"

"Is this Jace Wilder?" a male voice asked nervously.

"Yeah, who's this?"

"It's Matt Rifkin," he replied hesitantly. "I was a senior when you were a freshman. We were on the baseball team together at Public."

Oh yeah, I vaguely remembered him. He was a tall guy, a little overweight but a decent hitter. Why the hell was he calling me right now? This was not what I needed.

"Yeah, I remember you – listen, Matt, this isn't a good time to catch up," I told him.

"I'm not calling for that," he said. "I just, I thought I should call you because I just saw Pepper Jones."

"What? Where?" I interrupted him.

"I work the front desk at the Marriott in Brockton, and I was going into the back office when I saw her come in a side door with Clayton Dennison."

I was already turning toward the Marriott, but I kept listening, my insides twisting with panic. "I wasn't sure whether to call you, but I know she's like, um, your girlfriend, or best friend or something, and she looked a little, well, nervous? I decided it wasn't my place, but then I got to thinking, and I got your number from –"

I cut him off. If he wanted to get in my good graces, be part of my inner circle or something, I couldn't've cared less right then. I just needed information. "How long ago?"

"What?"

"When did you see her?" I thought I might be shouting or growling but it didn't matter.

"Oh, um, maybe half an hour ago."

"I'll be there in two minutes. Find out what room he's in and go in there. Get security."

"Dude, I don't really have the authority..."

"Just do it!" I yelled. "She's in trouble and he's dangerous."

I hung up and focused on getting there as fast as possible.

Chapter Forty

PEPPER

"Can I go to the bathroom first? I'm, well, I'm on my period." I try to fake embarrassment, but he's not buying it. I've never been a very convincing liar and I'm wishing more than anything I'd worked on the skill. "And I really have to pee," I add.

He rolls his eyes and follows me to the bathroom, and it takes a moment before I realize he's planning to stand there while I go. I didn't really have a plan, I guess I thought I might be able to text someone, but just then there's a knock at the door, and Clayton immediately covers my mouth with his hand before I even think to yell.

The next sixty seconds happen so fast, I have no time to react. Someone tries to open the door but is blocked by the dead bolt. Clayton's hand tightens around my mouth and I'm not only unable to speak, but I'm also having difficulty breathing. I don't think he realizes he's covering my nostrils, too. I attempt to claw at his hands but he squeezes a huge arm around my own, and I'm stuck in place, trying desperately to move my head back and forth to communicate that I can't breathe, but Clayton's focused on the door. There's a loud crash, and suddenly his hands are off of me, and I gasp for air.

Clayton darts for someone and I'm blinking through blurry eyes. There's a guy standing there, mouth agape, wearing a Marriott polo shirt, and he's watching something. In slow motion, I turn to see Clayton pinning Jace to the ground, but in the next moment Clayton's crashed into the television, and Jace is over him.

Their movements are violent and furious and I just stand there, in some sort of shock, unable to speak or react, for who knows how long, before uniformed officers are there, breaking them up. When they start to put Jace in handcuffs, I snap out of it.

"No! No, he's the one who saved me," I blurt out, but no one's listening. A strong arm goes around me, and there's Frankie, the biggest person in the room, holding onto me.

"Shhh... Pepper, we'll get this worked out, okay? Don't worry."

The guy in the polo shirt and Frankie talk to the three officers, and the room feels much too crowded, like we might not all get enough oxygen if someone doesn't step out. Clayton's gaze burns through me but I refuse to look at him. What is he thinking now? How could I have been so blind about him? I'm starting to shake, knowing he's watching me, and even though he's handcuffed and restrained by an officer, I don't want to be anywhere near him, and I push away from Frankie until I'm alone in the hallway, sucking in air in giant gulps.

When I finally look up, I realize there are a couple of people poking their heads out of the hotel rooms curiously, wanting to see the show. I'm tempted to run and hide because I don't want these strangers using my life, the horror that just happened, almost happened, as a juicy story to tell to their friends. I don't want them to see Jace and recognize him and say things about him that aren't true. But then he comes out of the room, looks at me and wraps me in his arms and none of it matters anymore.

———

At my urging, Jace plays in his last collegiate home game only a couple of hours later. We're asked a lot of questions by the Brockton police until Detective Marshall shows up and asks all of the same questions again. Clayton must have been escorted out when I was in Jace's arms, because I didn't see him again. I actually went to the game with my housemates, and though they got a short rundown on what happened, we cheered and acted almost normal. I didn't take my eyes off Jace the whole game, somehow afraid he'd disappear if I did.

But I've got him alone now, finally, and we're lying on our backs on my bed at Shadow Lane.

"You can get rid of the air mattress at purple house," I tell him. We're both staring at the ceiling, which makes it easier to talk. Otherwise I'd just crawl into him and forget about the important words I need to say.

"Yeah?"

"Yeah, I was going to tell you that before any of that happened today. After my run, I guess I had an epiphany. And then, when I was alone in the hotel room with Clayton, I had another one."

He reaches for my hand. "You've had quite a day, huh? Tell me about your epiphanies."

"This summer, you said something about fear, and you were right. At races, when I hit that point where it's really hard, I haven't been pushing through it like I used to."

"But you did today, didn't you?"

"Yeah, and it was awesome. I don't know, it isn't the same thing with us, but it just seems like it's time to stop hesitating and asking the 'what-ifs.' There's always a chance that something will happen, it always seems to with us, but I want to go for it anyway."

"Are the 'what-ifs' about me? Do you think I'll hurt you again?"

"That brings me to my other epiphany," I say, turning to face him now. "See, I've always had this weird feeling about Clayton. He made me uneasy and I couldn't pinpoint why, but I didn't trust him. He'd never done anything specifically to me that would cause me to be wary of him. At least, nothing I was aware of. But it was just this feeling."

Jace's hand is squeezing mine hard, and I realize I need to get to the point to put him out of his misery. "And with you, it's somehow the opposite. My gut feelings for you are good ones, and I get all happy when I'm with you even though I know I shouldn't. Even though you've given me a lot of reasons not to trust you, I can't help but trust you anyway."

"You trust me?"

"Of course I do. Can't you see that?"

"But you've been different with me. Not as open. And with Veronica — you believed her, didn't you? Until Clayton told you he set it up."

"No, I don't think I ever believed her, Jace. And I've tried to keep you at a distance because I was afraid you'd hurt me, but I've always trusted you."

"That doesn't make sense. You're saying you didn't trust me not to hurt you."

"Okay, yeah, maybe that part is right, but I trust you in every other way."

Jace closes his eyes briefly, and he looks anguished, but I don't understand why. Aren't I delivering good news, the news he's been hoping to hear?

"What will it take for you to trust me in every way?"

"I don't know. Time, I guess. I suppose I've still been angry with you, and I think I'm letting that go, too, especially now that I think I actually *want* to let it go. It's been a little bit of a protective armor, maybe, keeping me safe from you." We both chuckle at that for some reason.

"You thought anger would protect you from me?" he teases, but I won't let us get off track. I've got a point to make.

"What I'm saying is that I want to get there. It won't happen right away, but it will eventually, and I'm willing to work through it. I don't think we can go back to where we were before Annie left, but maybe if we work through it we'll get to an even better place someday."

And that's enough for now, apparently, because Jace decides we've had enough talking for the night, and I'm right there with him.

Chapter Forty-One

JACE

She had said it would take time, but her epiphanies had definitely made her open up more, and Pepper was being honest with me about everything again. Her fears and hopes for upcoming Nationals, her hesitations about Bunny getting married, the developments in her friends' relationships. She was happiest when her friends were happy, but I could tell she had been carrying some loneliness with her too. We both had, and now that she was "going for it" with our relationship again, I know I felt lighter and I think she was more carefree too.

That could've just been because the Clayton/Wolfe saga was resolved. Or at least resolving. Wolfe had shown up at the Denver police station the day after he told me about Clayton. Pepper didn't recant her testimony, but when he said he'd been paid by Clayton to essentially act out the whole thing, he wasn't charged with attempted kidnapping or sexual assault because he didn't have the intent to actually do any of that. I didn't end up turning over any of the other evidence I had on him because who knows, I might still need to use it someday. Wolfe pleaded guilty to assault and got some time, but Clayton's case is still underway. It goes back to Savannah Hawkins's case, and if he can't work out a deal, there might be a trial. No one wants that. Not the Rockies, and definitely not me or Pepper. We'd have to testify and so would Frankie and possibly others. A lot of the story had been kept under wraps, but enough of it had leaked to get some media attention. If it went to trial, it would be the media story of the year, nationwide most likely.

But it was like Pepper said – shit would come our way, it always did, and we were going to roll with it, together, when it hit. In the past, it seemed like we were always wondering if we could make it, especially when shit hit the fan, but she was right when she said it was time to stop hesitating and second-guessing and just go for it. I was hoping she could do that today at Nationals on the course, and then again later, with me.

Chapter Forty-Two

PEPPER

"I can't believe I'm warming down with an All-American," Jace says. We're jogging around the course after the race, just the two of us. He showed up in running clothes, and insisted on jogging with me.

"Well, technically I already warmed down with my teammates and I'm just humoring you."

"I wanted to see what it was like to run the course," he insists. When we get to the top of a hill in the woods, he tugs me to the side of the trail behind a tree for a kiss. "I'm so proud of you, Pepper."

"It's a good feeling, and I'm so glad you were able to come watch. I can hear you when you're cheering. Did you know that?"

"Yeah, because you always get this real determined look on your face and start passing people," he says smugly.

I roll my eyes. "You're so full of yourself. Come on, I don't want to miss the award ceremony." I'd only needed to place in the top twenty-five to get All-American, but I'd finished third. Next year, I'd go for the win.

"Hang on, I've just got to ask you one thing first, but you can answer whenever you want, okay?"

"Okaaay," I say uncertainly, wondering what game he's playing. But then he bends down on one knee and I think he's going to fix his shoelace or something until he reaches into his waistband and holds out a ring.

I'm frowning, confused. Did he just find that somewhere, or...? Wait, no way.

"Will you marry me, Pepper Jones?"

"What, now?" I'm incredulous. We're so young, and he's graduating, and we're only just figuring things out again.

He doesn't waver though. "I'd do it today, if you wanted, but I'll wait as long as you want. Just don't make me wait too long, okay?"

"You're proposing to me," I stammer stupidly.

He smiles, still on one knee, holding the ring between his fingers. "You need to know you're it for me. You have been for a really long time, and that's not going to change. Whether you start wearing this ring now or in ten years, or twenty, but I hope not, I'm going to be in love with everything about you. I want all the crazy that comes our way to be together. I want you by my side no matter how my football career pans out, and I want to be there for you when you chase your dreams racing. I know what I want and I know it's you."

"Did you practice that?" I murmur. "It's really nice." Eloquent, even, and I want to etch each word into my memory. I'm trying to memorize this image of him on one knee in a patch of leaves, the wind swirling around us, but my emotions take hold and I throw myself at him, knocking him on his back. I grab the ring from him and slide it onto my finger and then hold his head in my hands and say, "Yes."

I'm grinning like a maniac when I accept my third place finish and All-American award thirty minutes later. I want to wave a flag in the air that announces my newly engaged status, but I settle for telling my teammates, who react quite appropriately, jumping and squealing and tackling me in their excitement.

Gran was definitely in the know because she's beaming when I find her after the award ceremony. "You don't really have to share your wedding day with me, dear, I just wanted to get you thinking on the right track," she says.

"We'll see." This summer sounds good to me. "I think we'd look pretty awesome walking down the aisle together though, Bunny Barker."

"Stop calling me that! I'll always be a Jones."

"I won't. This time next year, I'll be Pepper Wilder."

Jace comes up to me then and lifts me in the air. "Pepper Wilder. That sounds like trouble to me," he says, but his voice is gentle and filled with awe when he sets me back down, and for the briefest moment, I see the future Jace and Pepper, chasing kids around Shadow Lane. I'd never let my imagination go that far before, but now, I'm able to see every bit of my happily ever after with clarity.

———

Gran throws together an engagement party as soon as the semester ends. She's been a whirlwind of energy since Nationals, talking nonstop about wedding dresses, wedding cakes, wedding shoes, and, well, weddings. My wedding, to be exact. I'm hoping after she throws this engagement party she'll settle down a bit, but I think I'd better have this wedding sooner rather than later or Gran will have way too much time to plan, which might not be a good thing.

Jace and I finish getting dressed and leave his bedroom to head over to the party with Frankie and Lizzie, who jump up from the couch when they see us.

"Veronica got kicked out!" Lizzie exclaims.

Frankie's smiling and shaking his head. "You'd think Lizzie would be satisfied with her getting kicked off the team, but I guess the girl deserved expulsion too."

Right before soccer playoffs, the coaches received an anonymous email with videos and photos of Veronica snorting cocaine, and a suggestion that she should be tested before representing the school in varsity athletics. She was kicked off the team a few days later.

"She was expelled for using cocaine?" I ask. That seems a bit harsh, given that a lot of college students do drugs.

"No, for cheating in not one, but two different classes," Lizzie says. "She used to brag about it. It was bound to catch up with her."

"Did you have any reason to dislike her before she pretended to hook up with Jace?" I ask Lizzie, who's never seemed particularly malicious before, though I can't say I'm disappointed that Veronica got kicked out for doing something that she deserved to get kicked out for.

"She's always trying to hook up with the guys on campus with serious girlfriends." Lizzie pauses. "You thought I didn't know, Franklin, but she was always throwing herself at you, and you were sick of it. You can thank me now, sweetie." She reaches up on her tiptoes to kiss him on the cheek, and when he blushes, I smile. That girl can always make Frankie melt, and seeing a guy that large turn beet red is priceless.

"I knew I'd put the right girl on the job." Jace leans forward to fist-bump with Lizzie.

"Wait, Lizzie, I never asked you about what you meant when you saw Veronica leaving the apartment back in late October. Do you remember that?"

Lizzie's eyes narrow. "Hell, yes. I'd left the apartment open for a minute to switch a load of laundry in the basement and she must have been watching or something, waiting for an opportunity. I thought she was after Frankie, and I didn't find out about her evil plot with Clayton until after the two of you got back together. I'm sorry about that. I totally could have helped explain those shenanigans if I'd known."

"It was stupid. I never really believed it, to be honest," I admit. Jace wraps his arms around my waist and lifts me in the air. "Hang on," I say through giggles. "I want to know what you meant when you asked her what she was up to 'this time.' Had she tried getting into the apartment before?"

Frankie and Lizzie nod in unison. "Yep," Frankie says. "Once before, Lizzie and I were coming out of my room and caught her coming in the front door, which we'd left open. The girl had been hitting on me, man," Frankie says to Jace, "so I didn't tell you. Didn't think it was about you. Sorry."

"Forgiven," Jace says with an ease that still seems uncharacteristic. But he's gotten his revenge, and he's got me, so really, what is there to be upset about anymore? Our past is just that: the past.

I tug Jace's hand. "We're going to be late for our own party."

Gran's throwing our engagement party at the Brockton senior center, where she has "connections" and was able to rent out the auditorium. She told me the other day that it's not easy finding a place that can hold over a hundred guests, and when she saw my reaction, she quickly backtracked, pretending like she'd only invited "twenty people or so." Right. Whatever, if Gran wants to invite every person I've ever known in Brockton, that's cool with me. Jace doesn't seem to mind either. Though it does make me wonder how many people she's planning to invite to the actual wedding.

"I think the last time I was here was with you, Jace," I comment as we pull into the parking lot.

"Uh, yeah, that was a traumatizing experience. You mean when Gran and Lulu dragged us to Bingo with them, right?"

"Well, it was really you who they wanted to bring. They'd promised some of their friends they could meet you," I remind him. "Didn't one woman in her nineties give you her phone number?"

"Two, actually. Dottie and Marge. They said I should call if I was looking for any work fixing stuff. But they were winking. It was really disturbing."

Lizzie and Frankie burst out laughing. "You remember their names, though!" Lizzie teases.

Jace shakes his head. "Those two were hard to forget."

We're still laughing about Dottie and Marge hitting on Jace when we step inside the auditorium. I pause in the entryway, and Jace takes my hand. The Bingo room has been transformed. Red and orange paper lanterns hang from the ceiling, and the tables are covered with matching polka-dotted tablecloths. The place looks amazing, and I find myself twirling around as I walk forward, taking it all in.

"Whoa," Lizzie says what we're all thinking. "If Bunny did all this for the engagement party, I can't even imagine what she's got in store for the wedding day."

"I knew the woman liked to party, but damn, she really knows how to plan one, too, huh?" Frankie says, eyeing a table in the far corner that appears to be adorned with cupcakes.

"Where is everyone?" Jace asks, and I realize for the first time that it's empty. We were told the party started at seven, and it's almost eight.

Just then, Gran storms in from the other end of the auditorium, and I blink several times as I take in her dress. Really, it's a gown. A red polka-dotted one with ruffles. She and I have always shared a love for polka dots, but wow, this dress is bold, even for Gran.

"You could have told me about the plan to coordinate outfits with the decorations!" I call out to her as she skips our way.

"About time!" she squeals. "People will be here any minute!"

"About that," I begin.

"Well, here's the thing," Gran jumps in. "This isn't just your engagement party. See, it's also my wedding."

"What?!" all four of us exclaim in unison.

"I didn't want you fussing about it, and I want your wedding day to be your own," Gran says defensively, clearly having prepared herself for an outburst.

"Bernadette Jones! You planned your wedding to Wallace without telling me! You tricked me!" I'm not sure why I'm angry with her, probably because she didn't let me help her at all.

"You had Nationals, and then finals, and really, I had so much fun. It's like a warm-up for your wedding! I've got so many great ideas. You know, cupcakes are really in these days, instead of a traditional wedding cake. And if you want to go with a polka-dotted theme, you can find all kinds of things on the internet without using the same stuff I did," she babbles.

"Gran." I try for a serious voice. "I'm mad at you."

"You can't be mad at me! It's my wedding day!" she declares, throwing up her hands dramatically.

"You're getting married on a Friday night?" Jace asks.

"Yep. Just a five-minute ceremony and then on to the party. Did you know that Wallace has friends in a rock band? We got special permission from the senior center to stay open until midnight. Hope you've got some energy for dancing!" Gran giggles like a little girl, and it's contagious. "I've got my dancing shoes on!" She pulls up her gown to reveal polka-dotted high top sneakers and ruffled socks.

"Bunny, you've got some serious style. You could probably start your own fashion line," Lizzie says, and as far as I can tell, she's dead serious about it.

"Yeah." Gran points her toe as she displays her shoes. "I've thought about that. Maybe I'll start with one of those pinned or poked interest pages. Lulu's got one of them."

"Are you talking about me?" Lulu, Gran's equally zany best friend, bustles in, her hair a blazing orange with a red stripe in the front. It changes colors monthly these days.

"Sure am," Gran says happily.

"All right, let's do this!" Lulu shouts, throwing a fist in the air, like we're about to start a football game or something.

"Lulu's marrying us," Gran explains. "We just need Wally."

"Right now?" I ask, suddenly inexplicably anxious. Gran's getting married! I didn't even get to prepare myself emotionally, or write a speech, or get them a gift.

"I'm here!" calls Wallace, entering from the door at the other end of the gym.

"I got my license to marry you, and the party's starting in four minutes," Lulu says with a glance at her watch. "Get your booty over here."

Wallace is also dressed for the occasion, with a cowboy hat, polka-dotted suspenders and a bow tie. "Check out his shoes," Gran murmurs with a nudge. "He wanted to wear his cowboy boots but I convinced him we should match." Sure enough, Wallace's high tops are the same as Gran's, minus the ruffled socks.

As soon as Wallace reaches us, Lulu is asking questions that she reads off a sheet, Gran is bouncing on her toes and answering them, while Wallace holds her hands and repeats his vows dutifully. The rings are exchanged, there's a sweet kiss, and just like that, I've got a new grandfather. I briefly wonder what I should call him now, but then people are arriving, and I've got no time to process that boom, bang, Gran is a married woman again.

Chapter Forty-Three

JACE

Bunny was one clever little woman. She knew Pepper would stress about Bunny's marriage and wedding and Bunny prevented that by throwing herself a surprise wedding party. The guests were the ones surprised.

The party was awesome. Everyone was home from school for winter break, so we had the whole Brockton crew out there on the dance floor. Wes and Zoe were all over each other; they hadn't seen each other in months. It was awesome watching my brother let go with her. He'd always played it cool, but something had changed because he didn't hide his fascination with Zoe by talking with everyone, being the life of the party he usually was. No, he openly watched her, sought her attention only, and gave his freely to her at the expense of others. Had I become like that, too? Or was I always that way?

The lovely Dottie and Marge were in attendance, and while they pointed out their dismay that I never called them, they noted how "smitten" I seemed with Bunny's granddaughter. "That one's a real catch, that Pepper," Dottie told me with a single eyebrow raise. "Hope you can keep up with her," Marge added. I was working on it, I told them.

Pepper had kicked off her shoes and was working the dance floor with Bunny, Lulu and Zoe. The band was playing an Ace of Base song that Pepper had requested, and the women were doing this coordinated dance that had everyone gathered around laughing and clapping. It brought me back to my senior year of high school, when I'd stopped by Pepper's apartment, as I often did. This same song had been blaring, and Pepper, Zoe and Bunny had cleared out the living room area to dance. They hadn't heard me come in, and I'd found the entire scene hilarious. As I'd watched Pepper roll her hips, wearing only a sports bra and running shorts, my amusement had shifted to something else, and my pulse had quickened. I'd wanted her for so long back then, and now, as the guests cheered and the music switched to Elvis, I finally had her. Forever.

As more people joined the dance floor, I moved through the dancing bodies, with one girl on my mind. When I got to her, I pulled her body to mine, filled with wonder and satisfaction at the feel of her softening in my arms. We'd grown up together, from kids to adults, from lost and confused to strong and determined. She was my redemption, and I'd spend my life being the Jace Wilder that deserved Pepper Jones. Because I knew now that I could be that guy, and that it was easier than I thought it would be, especially with her looking at me like she was, like I was all she'd ever wanted. Like maybe, I made her better, stronger, too.

Chapter Forty-Four

PEPPER

Six Months Later

"Dude, in nine hours you'll be Pepper Wilder," says Lexi.

Zoe sounds it out. "Pepper. Jones. Wilder. Yeah, it's totally got the professional runner vibe to it," she declares.

We're running on my favorite trail in Brockton, winding up the single track behind Shadow Lane, with Dave weaving between our legs. He knows it's a big day.

"You think you'll go with Adidas or Nike?" Lexi asks.

"I don't know. A rep from Brooks contacted me a couple of days ago, so I've got to do some research I guess." I've still got another year of college running ahead of me, but after a podium finish at Nationals and then adding an indoor 5K and an outdoor 10K title during track seasons, I'm going to have some options when I graduate. Choosing a sports agent, professional coach, contract, and training group is even more complicated than choosing a college.

"Doesn't Brooks have an elite program in Cleveland?" Zoe asks. Jace had been drafted by the Cleveland Browns, and after our honeymoon he was moving to Ohio.

"I'm not sure, but even if they do, Jace might switch teams after a year."

I know it isn't going to be easy being apart, but I also know we'll figure it out. I can train just about anywhere when I graduate, and with all the traveling Jace will be doing in the NFL, his home base isn't so important. In many ways, the timing with Gran marrying Wallace was ideal. The two of them are planning on driving all over the country in an RV after I graduate, and maybe it will be good for me to get out of Brockton for a bit. We'll be back, I'm sure of that.

"Long distance has its perks," Zoe assures me.

"Such as?" Lexi asks. She's staying in Brockton with Brax, unsure what she wants to do with her life. It doesn't seem to bother her that her future is uncertain, and I'm trying to let her attitude rub off on me a little. As long as it includes running and Jace, I don't need to figure out all the details just yet.

"Well, let's just say, abstinence makes the lust grow fonder, or something like that," Zoe says with a giggle. Oh man, Wes really is like a brother to me in some ways already, and would soon be my brother-in-law. I don't want to think about him and lust.

On our way back to Shadow Lane, we pass Gran and Jim walking briskly. When Jace and I told Gran that Jim would start jogging if she did, she got permission from her doctor to do "fast walking" and she declared that, given her bad hip, it counted as jogging. Jim agreed to walk with her most mornings, and I actually caught him running on the bike path alone one afternoon a few weeks ago, but he told me not to tell Jace yet, because he wanted to get in better shape first.

Jim will be walking me down the aisle today, and Gran, well, she's my matron of honor. When I couldn't decide between Lexi and Zoe, Gran stepped up to the plate. She even organized my bachelorette party, which really wasn't all that surprising to anyone. I was a little worried we'd get some weird exotic strippers dressed as tigers or something, but Lexi and Zoe, my ever-dutiful bridesmaids, kept her in check, apparently.

"We'll be by to pick you up in an hour for hair and makeup, chica!" Lexi calls as the two of them continue jogging to Zoe's house and Dave and I head up to our apartment.

I'm expecting a moment alone, perhaps my only one of the day, but my fiancé is sitting on the kitchen counter.

"Jace! You are not supposed to see me today! What do you think

you're doing here?" My outrage is an act. I'm thrilled to see him. I'd
rather have a moment alone with him than by myself anyway.

He doesn't answer, just hops down and lifts me up, so I wrap my
legs around his waist like a monkey. I'm sweaty and gross, but he
doesn't seem to mind. "Give me a break. I wanted to see my beautiful
bride."

"You better not have gone in my room," I warn. My dress is lying
out, wrapped in plastic.

"Nope, just scrounged around the kitchen, ate some muffins."

He brushes his lips against mine before setting me down. "You all
packed for the beach?" I ask.

"No, we don't leave until tomorrow."

"Yeah, but the flight is first thing in the morning."

"I just need flip-flops and a bathing suit, right?"

"Maybe a tee-shirt or two," I add. He can spend the week in a
bathing suit, I don't really care. We're going to Costa Rica and it will
be my first time out of the country. Jace asked me where I wanted to
go on our honeymoon and when I said the beach, he planned the
entire thing. I don't even know where we're staying. I guess having an
NFL salary has its perks. He hasn't even had a practice yet and he's
already gotten a paycheck.

"Jace, do you wish your mom was coming today?" It's not a question
I would normally bring up with him, but we've made a point of talking
about the hard things. I want to know how he's feeling about not
inviting her.

"No," Jace tells me easily, leaning against the fridge. "Everyone in
my real family, the family I chose, will be there, and that's what
matters."

"We have a big family, don't we?" By blood, it's tiny: one person for
me, and two for Jace (well, three including Annie... but we don't). But
with all of our friends from high school, college, cross country, track,
football... there's no shortage of love.

"And we're just going to keep growing," Jace says, stepping closer to
me again.

At first, I think he means with his new teammates, and my future
professional running friends, but then it hits me. I'll admit, I'd imag-

ined kids with Jace but only in a very faraway imaginary world. Now, it's a concept that we can make a reality someday. I grin.

"I can't even picture you holding a little baby," I blurt out with a giggle, because as I say it, the image of him cradling a tiny bundle pops into my head, and I kind of love it.

"I can totally picture you pregnant," he admits, almost teasing but a little too serious for my liking. He's rubbing my belly playfully when Gran and Jim walk in, both of their eyes zeroing in on Jace's hand on my stomach.

It's silent for a beat, and I contemplate messing with them, but their nerves are already on edge, so I can't bring myself to do it. "Don't worry guys, you won't have any baby Wilders for at least another ten years," I reassure them.

"Ten years!" Jace argues. "I was hoping to knock you up on the honeymoon!"

Jim looks a little pale at that comment, but Gran slaps Jace on the back in encouragement.

"Did you know that twins run in the family?" she asks. I think she's lying, because I haven't heard anything about twins before.

"Okay guys, time to get out so I can get beautiful." I shove Jace away. My bridesmaids will be here soon and I need to shower.

"You can marry me just like that if you want," Jace tells me, lingering by the door.

"I suppose I should warn you, I have a pretty sweet pair of dancing shoes that don't really match my dress, but I'm wearing them anyway."

"Polka-dotted track shoes! Special-ordered on the internet jungle. You can find anything on that internet store these days."

"She means Amazon," I clarify.

"Are you walking down the aisle in your track uniform, too?" Jace asks.

"Yep. A lacy white one."

"Is she being serious?" Jim sounds a little worried.

I laugh. "No way. That one's just for the after party," I joke. I may be wearing polka-dotted track shoes to my wedding, but I've got a normal wedding dress to go with it.

Jace and Jim are halfway down the hallway when Jace comes back through the front door and smashes his lips against mine. "Best day of my life, and it's only eight AM."

"And you're not even a morning person," I add.

"Love you like crazy," he whispers, holding my face in his hands.

"Always have, always will," I respond, before shoving his chest and turning to get ready for my wedding. Whatever comes our way, we'll face it together. I'm ready to take on all the ups and down, the highs and lows, of being Pepper Jones Wilder.

BOOKS BY ALI DEAN